Y0-DWM-843

LASER TROUBLE

"Space welding is very dangerous and takes practice," advised Dr. Thompson to Nathan and his Alpha team. "In this simulation, the laser is rigged in a vacuum room separated by a glass wall. If you miss the target, the beam could cut through the glass and kill us all in the explosion, so be careful."

"No problem," Gen broke in. "Let's get going."

His teammates Lanie and Noemi took their positions by the computer-operated mechanical hands and Gen sat behind the laser console. As the girls moved the two sheets of metal into position, Gen activated the tight beam to weld them together.

Suddenly, the laser spun out of control, hitting the sheets off mark and spraying red hot blobs of metal on the floor.

"It doesn't respond," Gen shouted, frantically tapping instructions on the keyboard.

"Shut it down!" Thompson ordered, but the laser beam moved on its own, heading straight for the thin glass wall.

JACK ANDERSON PRESENTS... **#2**

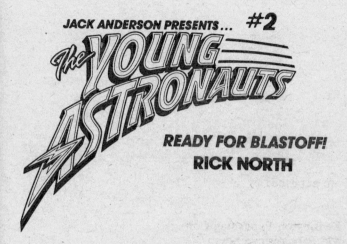

The YOUNG ASTRONAUTS

READY FOR BLASTOFF!
RICK NORTH

ZEBRA BOOKS
KENSINGTON PUBLISHING CORP.

RL 5.6, IL age 10 and up

ZEBRA BOOKS

are published by

Kensington Publishing Corp.
475 Park Avenue South
New York, NY 10016

Copyright © 1990 by Jack Anderson

All rights reserved. No part of this book may be repro-
duced in any form or by any means without the prior written consent of the Publisher, excepting brief quotes used in
reviews.

First printing: September, 1990

Printed in the United States of America

To John Peel, who helped more than can be known.

Prologue

The thunder behind and below them built up, slamming the seven passengers back into their padded couches. Balanced on a tail of flame almost six hundred feet long, the space shuttle slowly rose from the constraints that had tied it to the launch pad at Kennedy Space Center for days. As if it were happy to be free, the craft began to slowly turn and align itself as it reached upward for the stars. To the observers below, it blazed majestically onward, riding its torch. To the passengers within, nothing existed but the weight of gravity pushing them into their seats and the roaring thunder of over five million pounds of thrust that the cluster of engines produced.

The seven youngsters were dressed alike in simple red jumpsuits, and were all just over sixteen years old. There the similarities ended. The final result of a selection process that had spanned the Earth, they were from very different homes and backgrounds. Now, however, their backgrounds no longer mattered: they were all destined to be the among the first Martians. The shuttle was carrying them up into space, the first step in their long journey.

The pressure on them increased as the rising shuttle spun to orient itself for the final leap. It felt as though all the ties that had once bound them to the Earth were finally being shattered. The youngsters were all silent — not that they could have spoken above the terrific din of the motors — and each was lost in his or her own private memories.

This was it: their good-bye to the Earth. Unless something went drastically wrong at some stage in the mission, none of them would be back to the planet where they had been born and spent all of their lives before this moment for at least another three years. And, most likely, if anything did go wrong, then it would be fatal. From now on, they had no one they could rely upon but one another. They were no longer seven individuals from seven different families; they were a single team, working together for survival.

Karl Muller had his eyes closed. He was waiting for the moment that he knew was coming and was dreading. He was waiting to be very sick indeed from the effects of zero gravity, as had happened in training only a few weeks earlier. Though he knew that these feelings would pass, it would be a miserable time until they did. He glanced enviously at his friends, none of whom were even the slightest bit queasy, but all of whom were lost in their own memories and thoughts.

Sergei Chuvakin lay back in his acceleration couch, feeling the power below on which the shuttle was riding into space. It would not be long now before the incredible journey in front of them would unfold. The training was over, and the real work was soon to begin. Below, the Earth grew smaller; above, the Universe grew larger.

He thought back to his days in school. There he had read the writings of Konstantin Tsiolkovsky, the quiet Russian schoolteacher who had worked out the theories of space travel at the end of the nineteenth century. Those books had formed Sergei's interest in the stars. One significant sentence had especially touched Sergei's heart: "Earth is the cradle of Mankind; but

8

man cannot live in the cradle forever." When Tsiolkovsky had written this, no one had even invented a working aircraft.

Now, thanks to the To Mars Together program, he was leaving the cradle of mankind. He was one of the pioneers who would be heading out into the nursery that would shape the future of the human race. But he remembered how close he'd come to being cut from the project. . . .

The shuttle shook slightly from the force of the rockets it was riding into space. There was a brief sound of the two outer tanks from the booster falling away, and the craft leapt forward again, freed of their weight. Not long now until they were finally in orbit!

Alice Thorne shifted slightly on her couch, feeling the surge of excitement rising within her. Almost on the verge of space, at last! Alice's mind drifted back to the time when she had been on the verge of dropping out of the course, uncertain of the wisdom of her going to Mars.

Now, as the shuttle shook beneath her, Alice felt a growing elation within. She had made the right decision. This was the life she had been born to lead! This was her future — here with her friends and teammates, and farther out on the surface of Mars. This long rise to Earth orbit was just the start of the longer journey. She was fortunate to be a member of this new pioneering team, ready to carve a home from the wilderness.

Home . . . Not the planet that she was leaving behind, but the destination which still lay many months ahead of them.

Noemi Velazquez felt very uncomfortable as the gravity built up. She had been expecting it, of course, but it still felt dreadful. She hated to think what it was doing to her face. She had to look totally gross. This rise to orbit couldn't be over soon enough for her. Then things would get interesting again.

She instinctively checked for her bag, and then smiled ruefully to herself. This was one trip that she was taking without

9

benefit of her car keys, her overstuffed make up case, and her credit cards. You couldn't use them on Mars anyway.

Noemi tried to settle back. She had her entire wardrobe with her on the shuttle — the equivalent of one small suitcase. Quite a comedown; she only hoped that she wouldn't miss the rest of her clothing too much. There was, however, one aspect of the whole thing that hadn't hit her until just before lift-off . . . Possibly the worst horror of all.

She would have to do her own laundry.

With mounting excitement, Genshiro Akamasu felt his spirits rising with the shuttle. This was it — the event he'd been waiting almost a lifetime for! He was on his way into space!

Far out!

Being blessed (or cursed, he sometimes thought) with a photographic memory, he could recall exactly what had led to his being here — and how he had almost failed right at the very end of the race to make it to this awesome finishing line.

Ever since he had been a child, Gen had been fascinated with space. Growing up in Japan, he had been raised amid the clutter of the electronic revolution. He had been given his own computer when he was five, and his first compact disc player the following year. Keenly aware of the edge Japan had in electronics and in its new role as a space-faring power, he had been drawn to science fiction.

A voracious reader, he'd made his way through everything he could find, in both Japanese and English. Then had come the films . . .

He would watch anything — Godzilla flicks, ET, Night of the Living Dead, 2001, Star Wars — anything at all remotely connected with space. And he knew, without a single doubt, that this was where he would be one day — out in space.

He had worked hard at it, too. Well, perhaps that was an exaggeration; he hadn't needed to work that hard. His photographic memory had gotten him top honors in almost all of his classes, and his understanding of mechanics and electronics had helped everywhere else. He had coasted along, accustomed to his place at the top of the academic heap, and had breezed on into the Mars project.

Then had come the crunch.

It wasn't really that hard for him to stay on the top, even there. His unfailing memory helped, and his other skills cemented his position. In fact, in some ways, it was too easy for him. He'd started to take things for granted, and this had finally caught up with him.

Now, heading for orbit, Gen smiled ruefully. It had been a wise decision to commit himself to the group. He might never forget a fact once he learned it, but that didn't make him perfect. Each member of the team had his or her own special talents to contribute. Together they were much stronger than they ever could be apart. He knew that it would take all of the group, working together, to survive the coming ordeals — the building of their ships, the flight through space, and the settlement on Mars. And he was ready.

Lanie Rizzo could picture in her mind's eye how small below the shuttle their launch area must now be. Kennedy Space Center, Cape Canaveral, and even Florida would be shrinking down as the space craft strained to leave the Earth behind. "Farewell, Earth!" she muttered. "And good riddance."

Lanie had absolutely no regrets at all about leaving behind the planet of her birth. It had never done that much for her, and she would never miss it. In particular, she would not miss the Kennedy Space Center and the nightmares that had haunted her there for the final weeks before launch.

His team was on the way! Nathan Long, the team leader, tried to mentally run through what was happening on the shuttle's flight deck as the craft sped upward toward the Icarus

11

platform. Somehow, though, he couldn't concentrate on this. Instead, he kept thinking of Suki Long. She and her team would be following in a subsequent flight. There was something about the girl that Nathan simply couldn't fathom.

She was pretty, resourceful, and very intelligent. On her own merits, she could do almost anything that she set her mind to. True, her team had finished up second in the class behind Nathan's by a very narrow margin. What drove her to do the mean and sometimes vicious things she did? Suki almost got their team kicked off the Mars program. He wished he could figure her out.

He glanced about the cabin at his six teammates. They were a good crew and could all rely on one another. The last few weeks had proven that. . . .

Chapter One

Karl squinted in the bright sunlight, trying to make out what was happening on the airstrip. It would be hard to find a place more different from his native Germany than Texas. Karl was used to dark woods, sparkling rivers, and the winding freedom of the autobahns. Here at Houston, there was a scant shrubbery, hot, blistering winds, and roads that seemed to stretch into infinity. He glanced at his teammates, and then tried to grin.

Nathan had picked up on Karl's unease. Nathan was an American, but Texas as almost as alien to him as it was to Karl. Raised in the Midwest, Nathan was used to fields of grass or grain and small, white-shingled houses, not superhighways and oil wells.

Lanie, the other American on the team, shuffled her feet uncomfortably. The heat had forced her to leave her beloved leather jacket back on the bus that had dropped them at this Air Force base near Houston. She felt undressed without it. It had been the best thing she'd owned for the years she had lived in the inner city projects in Chicago. She'd grown up almost

13

alone and friendless, and had always looked out for herself, never being able to rely on others for help. Now she found herself a part of the team, wondering if she would ever really fit in. Could she ever bring herself to trust the others with her life?

Beside her, Sergei stood almost rigidly to attention. Soviet by birth, he was so fluent in English that it was easy to forget that his mother tongue was Russian. He was a fine student but had a weakness for pretty girls. Thankfully, he treated the three girls on the team as more like family than prey for his glib tongue and boyish good looks.

Alice shifted uncomfortably. The heat was making her sweat again. New Zealand had never been like this, even when she was working on the family farm. There, the air had not been this humid; here, she was constantly sweating. And uncomfortable. *At least people could live relatively unprotected in Texas — but not on Mars,* she thought. *It would be cool enough up there . . .*

Gen shaded his eyes with one hand and grinned out over the runway at the waiting aircraft. He was really looking forward to this trip! It might even give him a few new ideas for his music. He had managed to set aside a couple of hours in this evening's schedule so he could practice his guitar. It was getting harder and harder to find the time for that. He might have to leave the instrument behind when they lifted off for Mars so he wanted to get in all the playing time that he could.

Noemi was the last member of the group. She was also the first that most people looked at: not only was she beautiful, with long, rich black hair and a figure to die for, but she was also the best dresser. It was easy for people to forget that her brain was just as sharp as her elegantly manicured nails. Noemi had long ago learned that being popular was more a matter of looks than intelligence, and she had both.

None of them spoke. As they watched, the tall, dark-skinned Dr. Thompson finally broke off his conversation with an unseen man inside the aircraft, and then walked back to join them.

"Just a minor problem," he told them. "Sorry for the delay, but we can get on the aircraft now. Follow me." Spinning on his heels, he led the way back toward the training plane, talking all of the while. Dr. Thompson was one of the three adults assigned to the To Mars Together project, and their team adviser. He was an astronaut and a specialist in astrophysics.

"This is NASA's Boeing KC-135," he told them, as they approached the aircraft. "It was originally designed as a midair refueling tanker for the Air Force, but this particular model has been adapted specifically for our use. We'll be up for about two hours." Abruptly, he grinned down at them all. "If your stomachs come down at all."

At the cabin door, they were greeted by a native Texan. His lopsided grin grew as he solemnly handed each of them a small white plastic bag. "Keep this handy," he warned them. "And be ready to use it at all times. They don't call this bucket the *Vomit Comet* for nothing."

Noemi laughed a little scornfully at that. "Sick joke," she commented.

"Yes'm," the man agreed. "They all laugh at that. Sometimes, it's the last laugh they get for a few hours."

"I've never been sick in my life," Karl commented.

"I'm used to all forms of travel."

"Glad to hear it," their host agreed. "But this ain't like no other form of travel—'ceptin' going on up." He jerked his thumb toward the clear sky. "That's the idea of this sim-yew-lation." He pronounced it like three separate words. "anyhow, I'm Lieutenant Burdell welcoming you aboard. Step inside, please."

Alice led the way up the steps, then paused in the doorway and just stared. The other six, impatient to get out of the sun, pushed her on inside. After a moment, they were joining her in gaping about.

Most of the interior of the plane was empty space. There were some regular airline seats at the front of the craft, but very few. Beyond that was the flight cabin, where the crew would sit. The rest of the plane was devoid of windows. And the walls were padded.

"What is this?" Gen asked. "An asylum?"

"It's been called worse," Lieutenant Burdell grinned. "But that padding will come in handy once we're aloft . . . Okay, grab yourselves a seat and strap in for take-off."

They walked forward, noting that they weren't the only passengers. There were four other people, three men and a woman, all fiddling with what looked like camera equipment. The Texan caught their looks of interest.

"We can't waste a whole flight just to make you folks sick," he explained. "We're running a few tests as well. If any of you feel up to it when we start, then the docs will appreciate a hand. But if you're . . . occupied, we'll understand."

Reaching their seats, the team strapped themselves in. Dr. Thompson did the same, but Lieutenant Burdell stayed on his feet. One of the ground crew slammed the door, and they were ready for takeoff. They could hear the sound of the engines being fired up, but as there were no windows, they could see nothing outside.

"Okay, listen up," the lieutenant called. "When we get aloft, there will be lights coming on down the walls. Whatever you do, don't touch 'em — they get kinda hot, and I'm a mite short on burn ointment, hear? Next thing: Parachutes are under the seats. We'll have a quick drill with them, just in case."

"In case of what?" asked Lanie.

"Well, it ain't never happened yet, to the best of my knowledge," Burdell drawled, "but the plane goes through some tough stresses. Theoretically, we could just tear off a wing. I'd kind of like to think you'd be ready in case that happens."

"You're kidding!" Alice said, more in hope than disbelief.

"Just a touch," he agreed. "But it's always best to be safe, so we'll run the drill." They could feel the plane begin to taxi into position as he continued. "What we're gonna do is fly the plane up to about twenty-four thousand feet. Then we start a steep climb up to around thirty-five thousand feet. At that point, the pilot points the nose down and we drop in an arc. That's when the weightlessness kicks in. It's not really zero gravity or anything. It's just that gravity is pullin' you down from the sky at the same speed as the plane is diving. So what you really are doin' is free-falling. But it's closer to space than floatin' about in the trainin' tank back at the space center.

"It won't last long — about twenty-five seconds till we

17

get back down to twenty-four thousand feet. Then the pilot will—hopefully—pull out of the dive. You'll feel extra weight then. We do about twenty of the trips, then take a break before we do another twenty." He grinned again. "Remember to keep your little bags close at hand. If you feel sick, use 'em. Anyone who misses his or her bag gets to clean up their own mess."

Nathan stowed his bag in his top shirt pocket, just in case. "Do many people get sick?" he asked.

The Texan shrugged. "Hard to say. There's no predicting it. Maybe all of you will be fine and love it. Maybe you'll all be bringing back breakfast."

"I hope not," Gen muttered. "It was hard enough to get down the first time."

"Now you know why the food's so bad," Lanie grunted. "Why waste time making the food taste good if everyone's going to throw it up anyway?"

"If one of us is sick," Sergei asked, "will that prevent us from going up into space?"

Dr. Thompson fielded that one. "Not usually. A lot of people get sick at first, but get over it quickly. The only thing that would cause us concern would be if one or more of you stayed sick."

"What causes the sickness?" Noemi asked.

The lieutenant shrugged again. "Mostly it's the brain's problem," he told them. "Gets some odd signals, and can't tell which way is up or down. You can't trust your eyes, and the balancin' organs in your inner ear go kinda wacko, too. Gets your brain kinda confused, and it shows its opinion of the state of things by making you heave. After a while, you get more used to it and your brain calms down. So does your stomach."

The aircraft gave a slight lurch, and the engine whine increased. They were heading down the runway now, and with a gathering of energy, the plane rose. They felt the familiar feeling of takeoff, and then the climb. After a moment or two, they were in the air, and rising.

As soon as it was allowed, the team unstrapped themselves and followed Lieutenant Burdell into the body of the plane. He explained the parachute drill and showed them the emergency exits, and then moved into the more interesting stuff. There were footstraps and handstraps throughout the cabin for them to hold on to during weightlessness. The four scientists were setting up their equipment at the rear of the plane, and Burdell advised the youngsters to stay away from that part, at least for the first few runs.

"It'll take some getting used to," he told them, "no matter how well prepared you may think you are. And remember this: Don't even *think* about fooling around. That can get to be very dangerous. Try and stay within reach of the straps, too. If you're floating about in the middle of the room, and the weight comes back, you're gonna collect some nasty bruises. Worse, you might land on someone and hurt them. Worst of all, you might land on *me*. I may seem to be easygoing, but I *hate* getting a kick in the teeth. So be careful, okay?"

They all waited, looking nervously around. Nathan wondered if he *would* be okay. He hated to think that he might be the only one sick. It would be a poor showing if the team leader was throwing up all the time.

Then the plane tilted back, and they all grabbed at

19

the handholds. The craft rose at a forty-five-degree angle, and Burdell hollered out loud. "Yee-hoo! Here we go! Brace yourselves, one and all!"

The plane spun and pointed downward. Nathan's head swam, and his stomach rose. It was like being on a roller coaster coming down the crest — and into a fall that had no end in sight. His legs, pushing slightly against the floor, went sailing into the air, and he spun about the handhold. His head almost hit the floor, and he pushed hard away in reaction — and let go.

He went sailing backward through the air, arms and legs windmilling. It was slow moving, but he couldn't see anything except what had been the floor moving away from him. He tried to turn in the air, but there was nothing to grab on to. Without leverage, he couldn't change his path and — he smacked gently up against the padding.

Someone grabbed his hand and dragged it to a strap. Clutching tightly at canvas loop, Nathan tried to hold himself still and look around. His stomach was still protesting, but he hadn't gotten sick. He felt a sort of giddy relief over this and moved his head very slowly.

Noemi was stretched out in the center of the space, her long dark locks streaming out in all directions from her head. She was spinning slightly and looking as if she was having a good time. Beyond her — where the floor had been — Alice was apparently standing still. She had her foot in a toestrap, and stayed in place — two inches off the "floor." She had the plastic bag to her face and was busily being sick into it.

She wasn't alone. Lanie, too, looking almost green, was using her bag. Only she was floating away from everything and tumbling. Dr. Thompson, skimming across the air like a fish in a tank, snagged her and guided her foot into a strap. Then she hunched down miserably.

The only other one who was having real trouble was Karl. He was heaving up, but his bag had drifted off somehow, and he was spraying the air. Feeling sick just seeing this, Nathan still noticed that nothing fell, but just hung in the air. It was disgusting, but he couldn't drag his eyes away. Then Lieutenant Burdell grabbed at Karl, hauling him to a strap, and passed him another little bag.

Suddenly the weight returned. Like a hand, it dragged at Nathan, pulling him downward toward the floor once more. The aircraft had come out of the dive and was climbing again. The forces on Nathan were about two gee, he knew from his studies. Since he was hanging from the roof by one hand, it was as if he had someone his own weight on his back.

He tried looking down, but his head started swimming. The added weight was making his brain think it had twice as far to move his eyes as normal. He closed his eyes, steadied himself, and then opened them again. Things calmed down.

The weight gradually eased off, and he dropped down to the floor again. His first action was to thread his foot into a strap, ready for the next session. Then he looked around.

Gen was grinning from ear to ear; obviously, he'd enjoyed it. "Awesome," he laughed. Alice and Lanie both looked rather weak but determined. Noemi had pulled a brush from her pocket, and was furiously trying to get her hair back into shape. Sergei was pale, but flipped a thumbs-up. But Karl was sitting down, the plastic bag still at his mouth. His free hand holding his stomach.

Then the plane started to rise again. They were into their second session. Nathan felt proud of himself for having survived the first unscathed. Then, as the plane peaked and started to fall, he totally lost it. Luckily, he grabbed his bag in time.

Chapter Two

After that second arc, things got better. Nathan started to get the hang of things as his brain adjusted to the new set of images it was getting. After the fourth period of "weightlessness," he started to experiment with flying. He found that by kicking off gently he could float through the air and arrive at the opposite part of the padded wall.

Then it became fun. Noemi had taken to the whole thing as if she'd been born in space. She bounced about, curling into a ball, and then springing out when she hit a wall. Laughing, she sailed across the cabin. Nathan even managed to high five her on one pass. Sergei finally beat back his waves of nausea, and joined in. Alice, ever serious, left them to play, and "swam" across to the four scientists, offering them a hand that they gladly accepted. Gen was playing an air guitar, standing on his head and then doubling up with laughter.

Lanie managed to get a grip on herself and joined Alice and helped load photographic plates. The only one who didn't join in was Karl.

Each pass seemed to make him worse. He had emptied his stomach long ago, and now just retched and coughed. He was getting weak, and even Dr. Thompson was beginning to get worried. Finally, the first batch of twenty arcs was over, and the plane reverted to normal flying. Lieutenant Burdell grabbed a small hand-held vacuum and then stopped uncertainly. Nathan walked over, glad to have solid floor beneath his feet again. The Texan looked at him and shrugged.

"Normally, we make whoever threw up clean up," he said. "But your friend don't seem to up to it."

"I'm the team leader," Nathan informed him. "I'll do it." He held out his hand, and Burdell passed him the vacuum.

Cleaning up the mess was not fun, but Nathan realized that it was his responsibility. He was getting worried about Karl, who didn't seem to be improving at all. Even Lanie, the next-worst affected, had recovered almost completely from her nausea. On the final pass, she had even dive-bombed Gen and tugged the Japanese youth's long hair. Now that gravity was back, she was teasing Alice out of her solemn mood.

Karl just sat huddled, in a seat, hugging himself and lost in introspection. Nathan didn't know what to do. He returned the vacuum to Lieutenant Burdell, and before he could make a decision on Karl, the lieutenant announced that they were starting another set of twenty arcs.

As the others became more accustomed to the lack of weight, Karl just huddled in the seat, his belt tightly fastened and his eyes closed. He didn't seem to get any worse, but it was clear that he was not getting any better. Nathan saw the worried looks that Dr.

Thompson was casting in Karl's direction. It didn't look good.

Finally, it was over. Lieutenant Burdell announced that they were heading back to the airfield.

"Just when it was starting to be fun," Lanie grumbled.

Nathan glared at her, and she quieted down. Alice went to try to comfort Karl, but he shrugged her off.

It didn't look good to Nathan. Dr. Thompson had mentioned that few people were ever washed out of the program due to space sickness—but it was starting to look like Karl would be one of them.

The trip back to the space center in Houston was pretty wild. Lanie and Noemi refused to settle down in the bus and relax. Both of them were hyper after the free fall, and wanted to get scheduled for another trip up in the "Comet." Sergei laughed at them, and Nathan could see that he was just as eager to be off again. Gen was lost in a private world, and Nathan suspected that it was one of music, as usual. Every new experience gave Gen inspiration. Alice was lost in her own private thoughts, but with a smile tugging at the corners of her mouth. Only Karl was completely withdrawn, huddled over, still pale. Nathan tried to talk to him, but the German youth didn't even listen to him. Shrugging, Nathan joined Alice and simply sat there, savoring his own memories of the flight.

He did notice, however, the frown on Dr. Thompson's face.

After dinner—another disaster dreamed up by the maniacs in the cafeteria kitchen—Nathan knocked on

Dr. Thompson's door. Hearing a response, he walked in.

The office was cluttered, filled with well-thumbed books. The only exceptions to this were the wall with the large windows and one small space for a photograph. Nathan recognized it instantly: the Crab Nebula. The angry clouds of colored gas looked very much like the pincers of a crab, but Nathan knew that they were really the ever-expanding cloud about a supernova, a star that had exploded almost a thousand years ago.

Dr. Thompson caught his gaze, and smiled. "Believe it or not," he said softly, "I was young once. One day I saw that picture in a book in my library, and I thought it was the most beautiful sight I have ever seen. Still do." He seemed lost in his memories. "When I was up on one of the shuttle flights, I trained the telescope on the Crab, and saw it in all its glory." Then he blinked, and smiled. "But enough of that. What did you want to talk about?"

Nathan dragged his eyes away from the picture. "Oh. About today's flight, sir."

His supervisor nodded. "You all did pretty well, I think. A few problems, but you'll adapt well to space." He seemed reluctant to mention the obvious, so Nathan did.

"And Karl?"

"What about Karl?"

"He seemed very sick," Nathan said, a lead weight in his soul.

"Yes," Dr. Thompson agreed. "In all my years of training, I've never seen anyone quite that bad."

"Is there . . ." Nathan began. Then he swallowed

26

and tried again. "Is there any chance that Karl will be cut?"

Dr. Thompson stood up, moving to the window. With his back to Nathan, he answered, "I'd be lying if I said no. Karl seems to be getting worse as time goes on. Frankly, I can't see any way that I can recommend that he proceed with further training."

"Then . . ." Nathan said quietly.

Dr. Thompson turned around, his face completely impassive. "To be honest, Nathan, I can't see any alternative at this stage. I am going to have to ask that Karl be taken off the program."

Chapter Three

Karl was missing at dinner that night, and later for the team's discussion. No one mentioned it, as if by ignoring the subject they could all pretend that nothing had happened. When Gen went up to the room that he shared with Karl, he found that the German youngster was not there, either.

Getting worried now, Gen began searching the building methodically. Finally, after about twenty minutes, he heard the strains of a mournful piano from one of the halls. Silently, he slipped into the room and saw Karl, completely lost in his music.

It was a haunting yet somehow light piece that sounded vaguely familiar to Gen. In this room, with the lights out, it was as though some ghost was playing, conjuring up the spirits of the past. As the music came to a soft, satisfying close, Gen applauded.

Karl glanced around, and then turned back to the piano. He started to pick, but then brought his hand down in a jumble of noise.

"That was rad," Gen said, moving to Karl's side. "What was it called?"

" 'Fur Elise.' By Beethoven. It's one of the first pieces any pianist learns."

"Going back to your roots, eh?" joked Gen.

"I might as well," Karl sighed. "There's not going to be any future for me here."

"I never took you for a quitter, dude."

"Don't patronize me," snapped Karl before reverting to his gloom. "Let's face it — I'm going to get kicked out, aren't I?"

Avoiding that point, Gen touched his teammate on the shoulder. "Look, let's worry about that some other time. You've got to be starving, and pretty well bored with your own company."

"Yeah, I guess I am kind of hungry. But won't the cafeteria be closed now?"

"Hey, the last thing you need when you're depressed is any of their food." Gen grinned. "I laid in a stock of some good munchies."

He led Karl back to the game room, off from the main cafeteria. It was barely more than an alcove, really, with a couple of arcade video games in it. No one was there, but the games buzzed softly to themselves, throwing colored light from their screens onto the dark walls. Fishing behind one, Gen pulled out a bag with a flourish.

"Taco chips!" he announced. "Cheese Whizes! And even a couple of chocolate bars." Karl accepted a handful of chips and started to munch.

Gen gestured at the video games. "How about a round of Space Zappers?" he asked. "Could come in handy if we're ever attacked by monster insects on the way to Mars."

Shaking his head, Karl took more chips. "I won't be

going, anyway."

"You don't know that. Besides, there's no better way to work off your anger than to zap up some of these little suckers. Give it a try." Gen stuck in a handful of quarters and began his turn.

Guiding the video starship through swarms of giant metal mutant flies, he started firing. The room was filled with the howls, explosions, and screams that the game generated, and Gen laughed as he shot his way through the attacking swarm. Despite his apparent lack of interest, Karl noticed how high Gen's score was getting. Finally, though, one of the flies managed to grab Gen's ship, and with a blinding flash of light, Gen's turn was over.

"Radical fun, but it's your turn, soldier," he grinned, handing control over to Karl.

"I can't play these games," Karl protested. "I stink at them."

"Just give it a try," Gen urged. Karl shrugged, and started.

He was killed in about two seconds flat. He snorted and started to leave, but Gen stopped him.

"You're not doing it right. Look, you gotta fire slightly ahead of where they are so they fly into your fire."

"You think I don't know that?" Karl asked. "That's elementary stuff."

"Wait a minute!" Gen said, a sudden rush of adrenaline pumping into him. "You *were* firing ahead of those beasties?"

"Sure. I told you I'm not stupid. Just bad at the game."

With an inner rush of conviction, Gen plugged in

another game. "Try again."

"But I—"

"Try again!"

Puzzled, Karl shrugged and did as Gen asked. Once again, the game was over in a few seconds as Karl's ship was demolished. "Look, I told you I stink at this kind of thing."

"Yeah! Boy, do you ever! But I think I know what's wrong with your playing."

"Wonderful." Karl sounded totally bored. "I really couldn't care less what's wrong with my playing. It won't help me stay on this project."

Gen couldn't keep the big grin off his face. "Don't bet on that," he advised his friend. "If I'm right, then you'll still be part of this hot team."

"So tell me."

Gen shook his head. "Tomorrow," he insisted. "You're getting checked out by the eye doctor."

Dr. Thompson came out of the health lab, looking tired but happy. He glanced up at the six anxious faces, and nodded.

"Looks like you were right, Gen. It turns out that Karl has a very slight case of astigmatism in his right eye."

"A what?" Lanie asked.

"Astigmatism," their supervisor repeated. "A slight irregularity in the lens of his eye. It results in part of the picture seen by his eye being out of focus."

Gen grinned. "I figured it was something like that," he said. "Karl was shooting at those space insects, but he was seeing them out of place. As a result, he

31

missed every shot, but always by the same amount and in the same direction."

Still baffled, Lanie shook her head. "Maybe I'm dumb, but I still don't get it. What's this got to do with Karl being spacesick all the time?"

Dr. Thompson nodded at Gen, who was eager to explain what he'd deduced. "It's basically the same problem. The reason we got sick when we were weightless was because our brains were telling us that we were falling, and panicking when it couldn't tell what up and down were. After a couple of trips, though, we got used to it, because our brains simply processed the new information and we stopped being sick. But Karl's brain was constantly getting the wrong information from his eyes. As a result, he kept getting sick, because he couldn't adjust to the new conditions properly."

"Right," Dr. Thompson agreed. "Our doctors are sure that it's just a matter of Karl needing a small adjustment in the one eye. Maybe a contact lens, or a pair of glasses. Karl already has a prescription, I understand, but his optician must have missed this small problem. Normally his eyes can adjust to the tiny distortion, but in weightlessness, with everything else to worry about, his brain can't compensate. Anyway, you're all scheduled for another ride in the trainer tomorrow — and Karl will have his new glasses. Let's see if that helps him out."

When they took off the following morning, Lieutenant Burdell was watching Karl, looking somewhat anxious. Karl was sporting a new pair of glasses and an uneasy expression on his face. The rest of the team looked almost as tense.

No one spoke much until they began their first ascent, ready for the first period of weightlessness. Then the plane's nose tilted, and they felt the roller-coaster effect again, falling down that endless drop. Everyone's eyes were on Karl.

He grabbed his bag, and threw up again.

Nathan felt devastated. They had all been counting so much on this working out.

Waving his hand slightly, Karl tried to talk. It was not a good time for that, and he had to concentrate on holding the bag to his face. Then the weight returned, and they were all pressed back against the padded cabin walls.

Not knowing what to say, the six of them all stared at Karl. None dared see what Dr. Thompson was scribbling on his note pad.

Gen finally reached out and touched Karl shoulder. "Hey, man, I'm sorry. I really thought I helped."

Looking a little pale, Karl shook his head. "You did," he finally managed. "That was nowhere near as bad as I felt before. I think it's just the normal amount of sickness."

Hardly daring to believe it, Nathan glanced over at Dr. Thompson, who simply shrugged. "Let's wait and see" was all he could say.

Then they were into the second arc. As he floated away from the "floor," Nathan realized he'd forgotten to anchor his foot. He was getting used to this now, though, and spun about in the air to face the way he was flying. If it wasn't for the worry over Karl, he could really get to enjoy this. As he touched against what had been the ceiling, he grabbed hold of a strap, and then looked back.

Karl had been sick again, but much less than the last time. Maybe it *really* was working out.

It took another four passes in weightlessness before Karl could discard his bag. By then there was no doubt: he would be all right. It was a while before he could join in the work assignments they were all doing, but before the flight was over, he had even mastered the art of using a screwdriver in weightlessness. At first, as he had twisted the screwdriver, his body had twisted with it. He had forgotten to anchor himself down—a common mistake. Then he had gotten the hang of it. By the end of the flight, he was really beginning to enjoy the experience. He was laughing almost as hard as Gen.

"Hey, maybe I should become a space consultant," Gen crowed. "Another successful diagnosis! Way to go!"

"Maybe you should watch your head," Lanie shot back. "It's getting crowded in here, the way it's swelling!" But she was as happy as the rest of them.

The team was intact!

Chapter Four

A few days later, the team's studies had been interrupted by Dr. Thompson. Sergei was glad of the break, having read just about as much as he wanted to on celestial navigation, and he looked with curiosity at the two people who had accompanied their adviser.

"This is Jessamine Jarvis," Dr. Thompson told the seven of them. "She works for a company that produces documentaries for the PBS stations across the country. And this is her cameraman, Al Hart."

Jessamine Jarvis was a tall, blond woman, neatly dressed. Her hair was impeccably groomed, her makeup applied with precision. Her blue eyes bore into each of them in turn, as if trying to measure their commitment and interest potential. The cameraman, clad in Hawaiian shirt and slacks, just smiled lazily, and without any apparent enthusiasm.

Seeing their puzzled faces, Dr. Thompson went on: "As you know, NASA is being jointly funded in this project by the United Nations. Each member country is interested, naturally, not only in our progress but also in what its money is being spent on. Miss Jarvis is here to film some of your training, and she will be producing a documentary that will demonstrate how well we are doing in the To Mars Together program. You will continue with your normal training, and she and her cameraman will accompany you."

Jessamine nodded carefully, so as not to move a hair out of place. "It's important for you all to just act naturally, as if I am not here. Just do whatever you've been assigned to do, and forget the camera. I'll try to keep my interruptions and questions down to a minimum."

"Now, just carry on," Dr. Thompson told them. "Miss Jarvis will begin this afternoon." Then he led the two journalists out.

Immediately, the team broke and started to talk and laugh.

"All right!" Gen yelped. "We're not only gonna be astronauts, but movie stars!"

"And she wants us to act like the camera isn't there," Alice laughed. "Right! Nothing out of the ordinary."

Sergei ran a hand through his hair. "Hey—how many girls watch this PBS network of yours? Maybe I'd better get myself a secretary to handle all the letters from people who want an autographed photo of me?"

"You mean you don't already?" Lanie asked, pretending to be surprised. "I thought you already had a hundred girlfriends."

"A hundred and seven," he answered with as straight a face as he could manage. "You forget, there was a tourist group through an hour ago."

"This might interfere with our training," Nathan said. "That could cause a problem."

"What's wrong?" Gen asked. "Can't handle being an astronaut and a star? What a nerd." But he grinned as he said it, to show he didn't really mean anything by it.

Noemi had been silent throughout all of this. Alice finally noticed, and poked her with an elbow. "Hey, aren't you excited about what's happening?"

"Mmm?" Noemi seemed to wake out of a trance. "Oh, I was just thinking I'd better go to the mall. I don't have a thing to wear that I'd want to be filmed in."

Before they could start in on that subject, the team heard the door open again. This time, Dr. Thompson was alone, and looking very serious. Reining in their spirits, they paid attention when he cleared his throat.

"I think I had better explain a few things to you. First of all, you might think that this whole filming business is a game —" He held his hand up when they started to protest, and they quieted down. "But you'd better work it out of your system before this afternoon. This is serious business for us all." He sat on the edge of a table, and gestured them back to their seats.

"You probably think that with the go-ahead given to the project, everything is fine. Well, it isn't. This entire effort is costing an incredible sum of money, and the bill for it is being directly borne by the taxpayers of the countries involved. And, as you know, no one wants to pay any more taxes than they have to. There has been, naturally, a lot of opposition to the project. You've probably not heard about it, but in most of the member countries of the U.N., there have been plenty of political campaigns run on the idea of cutting funds for the To Mars Together program and saving everyone a lot of tax dollars.

"We're not very happy with all of this, but thankfully it seems to be still a minority thinking this. The majority still sees the establishment of a working Mars base as being the best thing for the human race as a whole. It is very important to us that they continue to feel this way.

"So I'm going to have to lay this right on the line for you. Miss Jarvis is filming the seven of you because you're the lead youth team for the project. There's going to be plenty of coverage of your lives from here on in. Don't let it go to your heads. You're not superstars, or teen idols, or anything like that. You're much more like laboratory rats. You'll be put through your paces, and left in public view.

"So far, you've all shown yourselves to be competent and inventive. You've also created more trouble for us than I sometimes think you're worth. But if you screw up here, it's not just your own necks that will end up on the chopping block. If you do anything — *anything* — that might reflect badly on the mission or on NASA, I guarantee that you'll be out of the project so fast you'll think that you'll make it to orbit without a booster rocket.

"And, worst of all, if you do anything wrong, then you could actually jeopardize the entire project. I know it's a tough position to put you in, but the whole future of To Mars Together hinges around you all doing absolutely nothing wrong while they have those cameras turning."

He stood up, and wearily ran his hand through his hair. "I hate to have to lay the cards on the table like that, but you do have to know what you're dealing with. Make it count." He turned and left the room.

For a moment there was a stunned silence. All their good humor had totally evaporated now. No one thought about becoming pinups or stars. Instead, the horrible prospect of being used as scapegoats for failure filled their minds.

"Uh . . . I hate to say it," Lanie muttered in a hollow voice. "But I think we'd be better off if we simply shot ourselves now."

"Hey," Karl said. "I know it's hard, but it's not *that* bad."

"Yes, it is," Lanie insisted. "If this documentary is produced and shown on PBS, it'll even get seen in Chicago."

Nathan shrugged. "I guess there might even be somebody in Chicago who watches PBS," he agreed. "So what?"

"You're all forgetting," whispered Lanie. "I lied to get into this project. Someone will see Lanie Rizzo on their screens. And they'll realize that Lanie Rizzo is Lanie Johnson, who was once arrested for car theft. And then where will this project be?"

After a few moments, Nathan managed a crooked grin. "Well," he said slowly, "I guess we'll just have to make sure that they don't get a good picture of you on the film then."

"Hey, no problem," Gen suggested, warming to the idea. "We can make sure Lanie's just filmed while her face is covered."

"Right," Lanie said sarcastically. "Maybe I should wear a paper bag over my head?" Despite her words, though, her tone sounded hopeful.

"Something like that," Sergei grinned. "For example,

we can have you filmed when we have the space-suit practice. No one would ever be able to recognize you inside of one of those."

Karl nodded slowly. "It's not going to be a problem, really, if we all work together as a team."

"And that," Nathan finished, "is what we're all here to learn about, isn't it?"

Lanie looked around at her friends and finally smiled. "What the hey," she laughed. "Let's try it. It's better than giving up. Besides, just how tough can it be?"

Chapter Five

They discovered the answer that afternoon.

As they gathered in the main entrance, Jessamine and her cameraman, Al, arrived. Jessamine swept in, carefully keeping on camera as Al panned about the foyer. She was casually dressed in a washed denim suit and a lacy white scarf. Dr. Thompson, looking somewhat scared, awaited her arrival. She thrust the microphone out toward him, watching Al get into position.

Al had a large camera slung across his shoulder which he constantly adjusted as he moved. A power lead led to the battery pack strapped to his waist. From the look of things, it was a pretty heavy rig. It wasn't hard to see how he had developed the muscles in his upper arms.

"We are talking with Dr. Lawrence Thompson," Jessamine said in her slightly breathless on-camera voice. "Dr. Thompson is one of the astronauts slated to be on the *Santa Maria,* and adviser to several groups of the young pioneers on Mars. Dr. Thompson, how can the member nations of the U.N. justify spending countless billions of dollars, rubles, yen, marks, and other currencies on a' flight to Mars when there are still so many people starving here on Earth?"

If he was taken aback by the nature of the question, Dr. Thompson hid it well. With a slight smile, he looked right at Al as he replied. "You ask that question as if there's a simple answer. We are not taking the money from the mouths of the needy to fund an idealistic dream — though many people have accused us of this. It's not a matter of money being taken from the poor to fund the ambitions of the rich. Most of the money for To Mars Together is being taken from the defense budgets of the countries involved. It's not a question of either sending one of these kids to Mars or feeding a starving person for a year. It's much more a question of sending a kid to Mars or buying another nuclear bomb. Which would you rather spend the dollars on?"

Sidestepping this question with practiced ease, Jessamine replied with another of her own. "But is this project simply a wild publicity gimmick for NASA with no practical aim or will there be some concrete end result?"

Again, Dr. Thompson smiled. "That depends on whether you consider the ultimate survival of the human race a concrete end result."

After a short pause, Jessamine prompted, "Could you be a little more specific?"

Aware that he had now taken the lead in the interview away from the antagonistic questions she had been firing at him, Dr. Thompson relaxed slightly. "By all means. At the moment, the human race numbers some six billion people. That sounds like an awful lot until you realize that almost all of that six billion is confined to a single place: Earth. If anything should happen to that one place, then the human race will go the way of the dinosaur and the dodo.

"There are a few hundred people who are not on the Earth right now. They live on space station *Icarus* and the Russian *Mir* platform. They might — and I stress the word *might* — survive a catastrophe that wiped out life on Earth. There are a few dozen more on the lunar base — and that is it.

"Now, if we can plant a human colony on Mars, then the situation will change drastically. Life on Mars will not be easy, but we propose to adapt the planet by a process called terraforming — literally, making a new Earth. If this works, then there will be two planets that can house the human race. That will make a disastrous end to humanity less likely."

Jessamine signaled Al to stop recording, and then turned to Dr. Thompson with a patently fake smile. "Well fielded," she remarked.

He nodded slightly. "I had been warned that you are not altogether . . . favorable to our efforts."

"Frankly, I think this project is a total waste of money," she answered.

"Hardly the impartial attitude I'd hope for from a reporter," Dr. Thompson replied.

"It's difficult to be impartial, Doctor, when you're spending so much of the taxpayers' money and risking the lives of so many children on this madcap idealistic crusade," she snapped back.

"The *children*," he replied, gesturing, "are over there. Why don't you talk to them."

She eyed him like a cat watching a bird. "I intend to."

Nathan looked at his team, and could see his own worries reflected in their eyes. He was beginning to feel like bait being lowered into a tankful of hungry sharks. This was not going to be easy.

"Now I know how the early Christians felt when they were fed to the lions," Alice said softly.

"Yeah, this woman is trouble," Lanie added.

"Hey, give her a chance," Sergei said. "She's just having an attitude problem."

"Right," Noemi smiled sweetly. "And you're not really looking at her legs, either."

Sergei blushed.

Then Jessamine walked over to them, trailed by Al. He held the camera down for the moment so they knew they were not being filmed. Putting on her professional smile again, the reporter faced them all. They could see she had a small computer screen in her hand that she referred to constantly.

"Okay," she said briskly. "You're the Alpha Team, right? The cream of the elite?"

"We're just the team that NASA selected for you to talk with," Nathan answered.

She glared hard at him. "And why do you think you were chosen?"

"We just score well in all of the tests, I guess."

"Well, we'll see how that translates on film," Jessamine commented. "But first, we'd better shoot some background. How are you assigned rooms here?"

"I share with Sergei," he answered. "Gen and Karl are roommates, and the girls all share a room." Seeing the next question the reporter would ask, he added, "The girls have a separate dorm, and there's a pretty strict curfew."

44

Disappointed that she had missed a possible scandal, Jessamine said, "Doesn't sound like much fun."

"Our building is the older one, and the rooms are much bigger," Alice said quickly. "They had to save space when they built the dorm the boys are in, and so could only build double rooms." She grinned. "Anyway, we girls are much more sociable than the boys."

"Dream on," Gen muttered.

"Well," Jessamine decided, "I guess that the best thing we can do here is to have a short guided tour around the dorms." She consulted her computer. "How about . . . Sergei for the boys and . . . Noemi for the girls?"

Grinning, Sergei nodded. "You picked the best looking?" he asked, preening himself ready for the camera.

"No," Jessamine replied icily. "The most foreign." She signaled Al to start his tape rolling. "Why don't you tell me about the building as we go down to the dorms?"

Taking a deep breath, Sergei moved ahead, gesturing. "This is the Johnson Space Center," he said toward the camera. "Named after Lyndon B. Johnson, who was responsible for its founding. It is the headquarters for NASA here in Houston, Texas, and . . ."

Nathan trotted along with the others, not interrupting Sergei's nonstop travelogue. He was certain that he'd seen Suki hovering in the background until a moment ago. Now there was no sign of her. He had no idea why the Chinese girl seemed to hate him and his team, but he knew that she was capable of almost anything. He'd have to stay alert.

As Sergei led Jessamine off to the room that he

shared with Nathan, Nathan puzzled over what Suki might be pulling. She had proven already that she was crafty, nasty, and creative. Her stunt with the car on the survival test had failed utterly, but she had made it clear that she would not leave it at that. Something inside her was driving her to make Nathan's team wash out of the program, and to establish hers as the primary team on the Mars project. Would she stoop to trying to sabotage them on film?

Much as he disliked the answer, Nathan was convinced she would.

They left the main building, trailing the still-chattering Sergei, and crossed the compound to the boys' dorm. As they worked their way through the corridors, Nathan saw Suki and Vikram Singh — one of her team members — dart down a side corridor. They'd been up to something, and Nathan had a strong conviction he wouldn't like it . . . whatever it was.

He caught Lanie's eye, and saw his own worries mirrored there. She inclined her head slightly, gesturing past the camera, and he nodded. They tried to edge past Jessamine, but the reporter held out a restraining hand, as if she'd sniffed trouble.

"Something bothering you?" she asked, breaking into Sergei's chatter.

"No," Nathan lied, as the camera swung to face him. "I just wanted to make sure that the beds were made."

"Don't worry," Jessamine said smoothly. "I think our viewers are probably used to teenagers who don't make their beds."

Completely oblivious to what was happening, Sergei carried on with his tour. They had reached the dorm room that he and Nathan shared by now, and with a grin, Sergei threw open the door. "A typical NASA student room," he announced with a grin.

Jessamine strode inside, one eyebrow arched. "I would hope not," she said dryly.

Sergei's face fell as he saw what the open door revealed. Instead of the reasonably neat room he and Nathan had left that morning, there was an utter mess. The bedclothes were strewn all over the room. Empty pizza boxes were tossed close to the trash can. And worst of all, on the cabinet by his bed stood several half-empty bottles of vodka.

"A typical student room?" Jessamine repeated.

Burning with embarrassment, Sergei was finally at a loss for words. Nathan hastily stepped forward.

"It's not how we left it," he said lamely.

"You mean someone cleaned it up?" asked Jessamine sarcastically, but she did signal Al to cut the taping.

"Someone has done *something*," Karl growled under his breath to Lanie. "And I think we know who it had to be."

Since she had also seen Suki skulking about, Lanie didn't have to ask. Instead, she tapped Sergei's arm and jerked her head back down the corridor. The Soviet followed her until they were out of Jessamine's earshot.

"Suki strikes again," Lanie hissed furiously. "She's trying to make us look bad."

"Yes," Sergei agreed. "And I will not leave this matter like this. I will have my revenge for this humiliation."

"I was hoping you'd say that," Lanie said. "I've got

47

an idea how we can get back at her. This afternoon we're scheduled for the simulator tests. So . . ." She started to outline her plan, and Sergei began to grin as it unfolded.

Jessamine shook her head as she thought about the taping. "I don't know if we can really use that tape," she finally said. "It's so obviously just a childish prank. No one would believe you'd all be stupid enough to show us that room and think it was normal."

Alice breathed a sigh of relief. For a moment she'd been seeing visions of them all getting kicked out of the project.

"We've got some real jokers in the program," Noemi said helpfully. "It helps with all the pressure."

Jessamine didn't look like she'd bought the excuse, but it clearly wasn't worth her while to pursue the matter. "Okay, Al, let's take a break. This afternoon, there's the simulator classes. We should get some good footage there. See you around, kids."

With a slight wave of her hand, she sauntered off. Al gave them another big grin, and followed after her, starting to disconnect his equipment.

Nathan let out an explosive sigh and collapsed onto his bed. Gen gingerly pushed aside the bottles and settled down on Sergei's. Alice and Noemi kicked away the pizza boxes on the floor and flopped down there. Karl leaned on the doorway, watching out in the corridor.

"We were lucky this time," Nathan announced.

"It's Suki again," Gen snarled. "What's with that witch anyhow?"

"I don't know," Nathan answered. "But that's not important right now. We just have to make sure that nothing goes wrong this afternoon at the simulator filming."

Noemi looked around. "Hey, guys," she pointed out, "where're Sergei and Lanie."

The others realized she was right. After a few seconds, Gen said hesitantly, "You don't think they're up to something, do you?"

"Sergei looked pretty burned by what Suki did," Alice said.

"Yeah, well," Nathan tried to figure out what he should do, but there wasn't anything that could be done. "Let's hope they don't do anything to screw up this afternoon."

Chapter Six

The simulator room was a large chamber in the heart of the building. Inside it was a full mock-up of the space shuttle deck. Wires ran from this to a complex arrangement of computers about the walls. The deck itself was mounted on a series of pistons that could move it in all possible directions. The controls of the shuttle were linked to the pistons via the computers. Anything that the trainees did at the controls would result in movement of the shuttle deck. The windows of the shuttle were all actually video screens, on which the computers controlled the pictures.

To get the young astronauts used to the controls, the computers could be run to simulate a number of different programs: blast-off, touch-down, or flights in space. The programs would run through, and crews for the shuttle made up from the teams would be put through their paces.

Each of the teams would spend at least one afternoon a week in the simulator rooms. Though they would never actually have to fly the shuttles themselves, they would be expected to help in flying the Mars craft. This experience here on the simulators would help them when the time came to train for the Mars piloting. Their work assignments on the three ships taking them to Mars would depend on their strengths and weaknesses here on the shuttle tests.

Karl was one of the highest scorers in the simulators. His love of driving and flying had translated into an ease with the shuttle controls. In fact, the only other person to even approach his ability on the simulator was Suki. She might be a menace to Alpha Team, but she was one of the best students in the program.

This was what Lanie and Sergei were counting on. Lanie had spent some time setting up her little plan, which had forced her and Sergei to skip lunch. When the rest of the team—along with Jessamine, Al, and the two other teams scheduled for the simulators that session—arrived, they found Lanie and Sergei lounging there already, looking very innocent. Both Suki and Nathan looked very apprehensive. No one had a chance to say anything, however, as Jessamine had Al start up the camera almost immediately.

"We are now looking at one of the space shuttle simulators . . ." Jessamine began as Al filmed. "Here, the young astronauts hone their skills in piloting an actual spaceship without endangering expensive in-flight equipment or their own lives. Let's take a look at one such drill."

She signaled Al to pause filming, and then looked around. "So, who goes first?"

"Well . . ." Karl began, taking half a pace forward, but Lanie jumped up.

51

"Suki's very good at this machine," she purred. "Why not let her team try it?" As Suki looked astonished and skeptical, Lanie continued: "After all, we're not the only team that should appear in the show, are we?"

There was no answer to that. Suki clearly didn't believe that Lanie's motives were entirely honest, but she couldn't say anything without admitting her guilt in the trick that morning. Jessamine apparently saw nothing unusual in Lanie's little speech, and she started to usher Suki and her team into the simulator.

Nathan managed to grab Sergei's elbow. "What's going on?" he hissed. "Have you two been up to something?"

"Us?" Sergei looked completely innocent, which didn't fool Nathan for a second. "What a suspicious mind you have. Lanie and I were just doing a little advanced studying."

There was no chance for Nathan to say anything else. He glared in Lanie's direction, but she seemed not to notice. She was pushing her hands further down into her pockets and ambling into the simulator to watch the taping. Nathan followed, with a dull, sick feeling in his stomach.

Suki was at the pilot's controls. Singh was by her, and the other members of her team at the various stations. Jessamine was crowded in behind Suki's seat, and Al craned about to get good footage of what would happen. Nathan's team stood just inside the shuttle hatchway, which they then closed behind them.

The computer then took over the program. There

was a brief flash on the "windows," and then a starfield appeared. It was as if the shuttle were in Earth orbit.

"This is all very impressive," Jessamine said, hardly impressed at all. "And no doubt expensive. Now what happens?"

Suki fought back her suspicions and began to explain what was going on. "The computer is creating the test pattern that we will run through. Whatever we do to these controls, the computer will analyze and then adjust its response. If I fired the small thrusters on the left of the shuttle, for example, the picture would move and it would look as if we were turning to the right."

"So the computer will react as if what you are doing is real?"

"Exactly. If we make a mistake, then we have a chance to see what we did wrong and to correct it. Then if we ever have to fly a real shuttle, we could be sure we'd know how to respond."

"And how old do you have to be to get a driver's license for one of these things?" asked Jessamine.

"There's no age limit," Suki replied as if it had been a serious question. "Just an ability test. You only get allowed to fly the real thing if you can handle the computer simulations."

Jessamine nodded. "Well, when will we start?"

"Now," Suki suggested, and hit the control to begin the program.

After a second, a series of lights started to blink amid the stars. "It's the 'Approach to *Icarus*'s program,' " she told the camera. "*Icarus* is the space platform that the shuttles have to dock with. The three

Mars ships will be constructed in orbit by the Mars teams, working from the platform. What we have to do on this run is to dock with the module on the *Icarus* and to avoid hitting any of the construction equipment or personnel."

Her fingers started to play over the controls. The star patterns began to change, and everyone could hear the whine of the armatures outside holding the cabin. The floor began to tilt slightly.

"Naturally," Suki said, "if we were in orbit, there'd be no weight at this point. At the moment, though, we have to put up with it. Hence the floor tilts when we maneuver." She tapped more controls.

"The control panels look complicated," Jessamine observed. "You don't have to watch them all as you fly in?"

"No," agreed Suki. "Most of them are sort of warning panels: If you do anything wrong, or anything goes wrong, then a flashing red light will tell you to check it out. As long as everything is green, then you're doing fine and can ignore it. There'd be too much to do if you had to watch everything."

The lights of the "space platform" seemed to be growing nearer. Suki tapped at the controls that were firing the "thrusters" to slow down the approach.

Nothing happened. Puzzled, she tried again.

Three red lights started to flash above Suki's head. Startled, she looked up and tried to figure out what was going wrong. Two more red lights came on. The lights of the "space station" were getting closer in and moving faster now. Even Nathan was puzzled, because Suki was responding to each problem correctly. No sooner did she succeed in getting one red light off, though, than two more began flashing.

Nathan heard a snicker from behind him, and in the half-light, he saw Lanie trying to stifle another laugh. Sergei wasn't even trying to hide his big grin. *So that's what they had been doing!* Nathan thought. *They had somehow fixed the simulator!*

"I don't understand," Suki cursed, trying again to adjust the controls. As she fought to regain control, the lights of the "space platform" were huge in the shuttle windows. Then there was a huge flash of light, and everything froze into its place.

After a moment's pause, Jessamine said dryly: "I take it we're now all dead?"

"That shouldn't have happened," Suki snapped, eyeing the controls with a blazing anger. "I did nothing wrong."

"Well," the reporter drawled, "you've managed to kill your crew and wreck the space platform. I'd say you failed the test. If you're an example of what they're sending into space, then God help us all!"

"Wait," Suki cried desperately. "Let me try it again!"

"Sorry," Jessamine said. "I think I've got enough film of you screwing up for now."

Sergei politely opened the main hatch for her, and the film team waltzed out. Al looked directly at Lanie, and winked. She broke out into laughter.

Suki spun about, her eyes filled with hatred—and something that looked very much like fear. "You . . . you . . ." she hissed, which only made Lanie laugh even louder. "I'll fix you for this, you jerk," she vowed. Then she stormed out of the simulator, her team trailing behind her.

55

When they were the only ones left, Nathan turned to Sergei and Lanie, who were lost in fits of giggles. "You guys are really stupid."

"Oh, come on," Sergei laughed. "She asked for it. Little Miss Perfect, out to make us look like clowns. Well, we fixed her."

"Yeah," Nathan snapped, "and you very nearly fixed the whole project." At this, the giggling duo finally began to sober up. "Don't you remember what Dr. Thompson told us?" continued Nathan. "This isn't a game—we have to make the whole To Mars Together project look good for the media. That little stunt may have humiliated Suki, but it also made it look as if NASA isn't training us properly. And how do you think Dr. Thompson would like that?"

Finally beginning to realize what they had done, Lanie and Sergei traded worried looks. "Well, we didn't think—" Sergei muttered.

"Right—you didn't!" Nathan agreed. "So from now on, you do nothing—*nothing*—to get back at Suki, whatever she does. You got that?"

"You want us to just let her make us look like jerks?" Sergei asked. "And let her get away with it?"

"No. We'll have to watch her carefully from now on. But we can't take a chance of doing anything else wrong. Miss Jarvis has two screw-ups on film so far. She has to get only good stuff from now on or else we'll all be dead meat, and the entire project might be canceled. We're walking on the edge of a long fall here, so we're going to have to keep our balance. And that means especially you two."

He could tell by the expressions in their eyes that they were blaming themselves more than he ever could do. He could only hope that their behavior from now on would somehow prevent Jessamine making a film that could kill the Mars project.

Chapter Seven

NASA had allowed the trainees to return to their homes over Christmas — with the promise of a very thorough medical examination when they returned to ensure that they had picked up no diseases that would disqualify them from space. Alice had had mixed feelings about this. Though her mother wrote often — long, rambling letters telling her how her younger brother Bobby was doing, or how the twins Joe and Lucy were growing, or how Dad and William, the foreman, had repaired the barn over the autumn — and Alice wrote back faithfully, it seemed as though New Zealand was already a different life. But it was also her roots.

Her father had picked her up at the airport, driving the battered old jeep that now looked to her like a relic from a museum. Not at all like the high-tech machines she'd been driving about in the Martian Rover tests. He had hugged her, grinning, and helped her stow her bags, but the ride back out to the farm had mostly been in silence. Neither of them knew what to say, though there was plenty both had hoped to talk about.

At the farm, though, that had changed. Dad had honked the horn almost constantly as they approached, and everyone came running out. Bobby, the twins, and finally Mom, wiping her hands hastily on the long apron she always wore. In a buzz of constant chatter, the kids had tried to get her attention. Mom simply grabbed her and hugged her tight. Then she'd stood her off and looked her over.

"They feeding you right?" she asked, a catch in her voice. "You look kind of skinny."

"I'm not surprised," Alice laughed. "You should see the junk they call food in the cafeteria."

"Well, you'll get good meals here," her mother promised. "Dinner in fifteen minutes, young lady!"

Bobby had insisted on carrying her bags up to her old room for her, teasing her all the way. He'd always tried to get her angry, but his teasing this time was mixed with something Alice had never heard from him before: respect. Her old room was unchanged, and it was hard to think that one of the other kids would be taking over here after she left this time.

She'd not be needing it for at least three years. And maybe never. It depended on how things went on Mars. So much had happened here, but now it was being left behind. Who knew how long it would be before she was back again?

Fighting down her emotions, she paid attention to what Bobby was saying. He had reappeared with a large scrapbook. "Been saving all the clippings," he told her, opening it up. Inside were pages of news stories, all carefully dated and ordered. They all dealt with the To Mars Together project. Bobby looked almost embarrassed. "It's kind of cool, being related to a celebrity."

She had never considered herself a celebrity! She was just following a dream, and had been lucky enough to get onto the project where a lot of others had failed. But a celebrity? Not her!

Seeing her amused expression, Bobby told her: "It's a fact. All the kids in my class ask about you. And three newspapers have called up, wanting to interview you. Don't worry, Dad told them they'd have to wait till after the holidays."

The rest of the afternoon had been spent in something like a daze. Mom had cooked up a huge meal—roast leg of lamb, baked potatoes and the trimmings, followed by apple pie, and pot after pot of coffee. Alice overate, thankful for food with some taste to it at last. Then she had let the twins show her all the changes made since she'd left a few months ago. There really wasn't anything new to see, but the twins just wanted time with her. She was glad of it. She'd probably never see them again until they were grown to Bobby's age. She'd miss most of their childhood.

Then, later that evening, she had left the house and wandered up to the hill behind the farm buildings. There she had sat down, and stared outward.

The stars burned, bright and clear. Almost out of reflex, she began to pick out the old familiar constellations—none of them visible from North America. There was Crux, the Southern Cross, its stars pointing the way to the South Pole. Close by it was Centaurus, with its sprawling shape enclosing Alpha Centauri—the closest star to the Earth. Beside that, the Coal Sack Nebula . . . Old familiar faces. She'd sat here so many times over the years, watching the constellations rise, and the glorious spread of the Milky Way in the sky. There, two smudgy patches showed the Megallanic Clouds — small Galaxies that were members of what astronomers termed the Local Group. Local, of course, only in relative terms. They were thousands of light years away, farther than anyone could hope to ever travel.

Soon she would be out there, away from the Earth and a part of that Universe she had always longed for. As far back as she could recall, she'd sat on this hill and wanted to reach out a hand and pluck a star.

Now she would. Only the star was a dream, and the place she was going to was Mars. There, the constellations would look exactly the same as they would from the Earth. The only difference would be that if she sat out on a hill on Mars, she'd do it in a space suit. And one of the bright, moving planets in the sky would be the Earth.

There was a terrible lump in her throat. Could she so simply turn her back on these hills and the people now sleeping in that house below? She hadn't realized how much she had missed them all until they had hugged her and greeted her home again.

Could she give that up for three years, or more?

The next day she had taken her old place at helping with the chores. Her father had protested, but Alice had insisted. Since she had been very young, she had had a series of jobs to do to help out with the work, and now that she was back for a while, she wanted to pull her weight. She fed the chickens, watching them scramble for the grain, and then helped William with a couple of repairs. The old sheepdogs, Mel and Sandy, had greeted her with their usual prancing and jumping, but it was Bobby who now saw to their feeding. It had been her job once.

She soon realized that the family had adjusted the chores to exclude her. By trying to help, she was actually breaking up the pattern of work.

They were getting along without her.

Strangely, this hurt her more than anything, that she could be gone such a short while and return to find that they could manage well enough without her around to pull her weight! Rather than get in their way, she wandered back inside, intending to help her mother with the cooking. As she passed her father's small study, though, she could see that he was inside reading a sheet of paper, a worried expression on his face.

She wasn't used to seeing him like this. Maybe it was just a trick of her memory, but she always thought of him as a strong, smiling person. Now, though, he seemed bowed beneath a weight.

She knocked gently on the door, and he glanced up quickly. He thrust the paper down onto his desk, and tried to bring a smile on his face. He didn't do too good a job of it.

"Is something wrong?" she asked.

"Wrong?" He looked down at the desk, and then spread his hands. "No, honey, nothing's wrong that you have to worry about. I'm just a bit rushed for time right now."

This didn't ring true to Alice, but she wasn't about to call her father a liar. Instead, she nodded. "I thought I'd give Mom a hand with the baking."

"Good idea," he said, sounding relieved. He gently ushered her out of the study, and closed the door firmly behind them. "I'll be back for dinner."

Alice made her way to the kitchen. Something was clearly wrong, and it was just as apparent that her father was in no mood to tell her about it. Which left Mom.

The kitchen was in its usual state of highly organized mess. Her mother was in the middle of making fruit pies, and the various ingredients were scattered about the huge table she mixed things on. She liked to have everything at hand before she began. It left the table cluttered, but it meant that she never had to go hunting for anything with floured hands. Alice pitched in to help roll the dough.

"Is everything okay with Dad?" she asked as she slapped more flour down on the wooden surface. She dropped the first lump of pastry down, and took up the rolling pin to begin working it out.

"I expect so."

"He seems to be worried," Alice insisted.

"Well, you know how it is. End of the year and all that. The bank's pressing him for facts and figures, not on mouths to feed and lambs to raise. Bankers don't understand the business of farming. They just understand cold hard cash."

It began to dawn on Alice now what her father was bothered about. "Is he having trouble making the loan payments, Mom?"

She nodded, and then held up a white, floured

hand. "Don't you go letting on that I told you. He didn't want to spoil your trip."

"It's because I'm not here, isn't it?" Alice said. "It's the money he's spent to send me through those technical courses. And now I'm just running out on you and going to Mars!"

"Don't be silly, dear," her mother replied. "It's just the usual problems we have most years. Your father will work it out. Don't worry about it."

How could she not worry? Though she helped her mother, Alice's mind was on the money problem. Her father had never said it, but he'd always assumed that the courses Alice was taking would enable her to help him run the farm better—not to get her off on a trip to Mars. Would he have been so willing to finance her training had he foreseen what would happen? Was she betraying him and her family by leaving them now?

Chapter Eight

That night, she sat on the hill again, staring into the sky. Low clouds obscured the stars, matching the emptiness inside her. She hadn't known about the financial problems facing her father. Typically, he had never said a word to her. He kept all of his worries bottled up inside.

There was a slight movement in the darkness, and her mother appeared. She still wore her kitchen apron, and there was the scent of cooking about her. Sitting beside her daughter, Mrs. Thorne smiled, wistfully. "It's beautiful out here."

"You can't see the stars for the clouds, Mom."

"But they're still there. You know what they look like, and where they must be. The clouds will pass soon, but the stars will stay forever." She sighed. "You know, I used to come up here, too, after I married your father. I loved to sit and watch the stars at night. Maybe you got that from me. I always wanted to be out there, somehow, in space." She grinned. "I used to pretend that I was an angel, and that I had huge, beautiful wings that I could spread. I could catch a breeze and rise, up above those clouds there and on, out among the stars. And now *you* can do that. I'm glad."

"I don't know if I should go," Alice told her softly. "I'd be running out on you all."

"Nonsense," her mother told her firmly. She put an arm about Alice's shoulders. "You've just got some daft ideas into your head."

"But Dad needs me here on the farm. You all do."

"Alice Frances, don't be foolish. Your father and I managed this farm for years before you were even born. We managed it well enough till you were grown enough to help out. Do you think we've suddenly stopped being able to handle it? Are we so old and feeble?"

"No!" exclaimed Alice. "But . . . the money, the loans . . ."

"I know," Mrs. Thorne said softly. "It's true. We do need money to pay off some of the loans we took out to help you through your schooling and studies. But do you think that staying here and working is making the best use of that education? If you stayed here, you'd miss the Mars project, and then you'd just have thrown away what we've done for you. Pay us back the best way that you can. Be the best astronaut on the team. Be the first person to get down in the soil of Mars and plant corn—or whatever it is you're taking out there. And raise it till it grows. That's what you should do. Anyone can work here on this farm, but who'll do your job on Mars if you foolishly stay behind?"

"There's always someone else, Mom. NASA's got

a lot of people on this course."

"I'm not saying you're indispensable, my girl, but you're the best they've got, I'd be willing to bet." She laughed. "It's not every farmgirl who can also be an astronaut, you know. And any number of fancy degrees won't turn an astrophysicist into a farmer. You've got to know the land, to have lived the land for that. It's in the blood, child, and the heart. It's not something that a university course can plant in your mind. And, besides all of that, what about those others on your team? Aren't they counting on you? What will they do if you leave the project?"

"I don't know," Alice sighed. "I just don't know." She started to twist her braids in her fingers. "It used to seem so simple, but now it's really gotten so complicated. I want to go to Mars—more than ever since I started the training. But I don't want to desert you and Dad if I'm needed."

Mrs. Thorne patted her arm gently. "Alice Frances, I won't pretend that there's nothing you could do to help out. Of course there is. But there's something much more important for you to do. Did Bobby show you his scrapbook?"

Alice nodded.

"You've given him—and thousands like him, all over the world—a dream, a goal. If a farmgirl from a small ranch in New Zealand can make it to Mars, why, then, surely nothing is impossible for youngsters if they set their minds on it. If you back out now, you'll see it as helping us out on the farm, but every one of those kids will see it as a dream dashed back into the ground. You've got to go on

67

and show them that there is a future, that there is something possible, that they, too, might make it to Mars—or wherever their dreams want to take them."

Alice looked at her mother in the gloom. Then she threw her arms around her and hugged her. "Thanks, Mom. I'll try—I promise that."

Mrs. Thorne laughed. "You've always kept your promises, girl." Then she pointed up, at a break in the clouds. "What did I tell you? Clouds always pass. Only the stars are there forever. That's the round of life."

In the gap, shining brightly, was Fomalhaut, one of the brightest stars in the southern skies. Alice felt contented; out there was where she belonged.

Back in the grind of training at NASA, however, Alice began to have her doubts again. Her mother had meant well, but she had planted a seed of doubt in Alice's mind. Having been raised a farmgirl, was Alice really cut out to be an astronaut? She constantly compared her performances on the simulators with the rest of the group, and began to notice areas where she was falling behind. She didn't realize that one of the reasons she was messing up now was because she had become so self-conscious about everything she did.

She and Sergei were on simulators designed to get them used to their controls of the suits they would wear to construct the Mars ships in orbit. Each suit was fitted with a small rocket pack on the back with which they could steer through space. To test their reactions, they were suspended in a room. All about them were video screens bearing images of the view from space. As with the shuttle simulator, the suits were linked to computers. Any instructions the two of them gave to their rockets would be used to change the video outputs and to demonstrate the results of their actions.

Her mind on the farm and her folks, Alice managed to crash into *Icarus* platform on the first flight. On her second, she ended up getting into the maw of a rocket as it fired.

"Fried," Gen's voice told her over the radio link.

"Oh, shut up," she yelled back. As soon as she was out of her suit, she ran off in tears back to the dorm.

Gen stared after her in astonishment. This was completely unlike the Alice he knew. "So what is wrong with her?"

Nathan shrugged. "Just moody today, I guess."

The breaking point arrived when it was her turn to be the subject of one of Jessamine's on-camera explanations. The reporter was still as nosey as ever, and had been filming them all day.

They were in the mock-up of the *Icarus* space platform, running through the tasks that they would be facing when they were really in orbit when Jessamine interrupted Alice.

"One of the questions that seems uppermost in the minds of the public," she said, "is, how do you go to the bathroom in space?"

Taken somewhat aback, Alice frowned for a moment, gathering her thoughts.

"Well," Alice finally replied, "it's a lot like a normal toilet on the Earth. The basic difference is that there's no gravity most of the time in space. So, nothing will fall on its own. If I were holding a pencil and then let it go in weightlessness, it wouldn't fall to the floor. It would just hang there in the air. You can imagine what using the bathroom would be like in zero gravity.

"The toilets we will use have to compensate for this. They have a constant sucking of air through them. It's not strong enough to stick you to the seat, but it's strong enough to get rid of the wastes."

Jessamine smiled. "And then what? You flush it into space?"

"No. The liquid part of the wastes are purified and recycled. The solid parts are dried and used as fertilizer for the plants. We can't afford to throw anything away in space. After all, we've polluted one planet enough. We don't want to begin our colony on Mars with a trail of trash in space."

Looking around, Jessamine asked, "Is there a toilet in this simulator?"

Alice nodded, and pointed to the clearly marked door. "Why? Do you want a demonstration?" She had had about enough of Jessamine.

"I don't think so," the reporter answered. "But perhaps you could show us it on film?"

Sighing inwardly, Alice logged off the computer she had been using and led the two newspeople over to the toilet. It looked like a small closet, with handgrips on the inside. "They're so you don't float away while using it," Alice explained. The only other thing in the small room was a tiny sink and suction dryer, to conserve water after washing your hands.

At Jessamine's urging, Alice sat down, showing how they would have to get into position, and then she pulled the door shut. For a moment, at least, she'd be away from the stupid woman and her dumb questions! There was a faint *snick* as the door closed. It sounded wrong to Alice's ears, and she tried to release it.

The door refused to move.

With a flush of sheer embarrassment, Alice realized that she had somehow locked herself into the bathroom—while Jessamine was getting every second of it on film.

Chapter Nine

"Is there something wrong?" Jessamine asked.

"It's stuck," Alice admitted, miserably.

Karl came to the rescue, having heard the final part of the conversation and realizing that Jessamine was on the trail of another mistake. Hastily, he moved to join them at the bathroom, gesturing for Lanie to come and help. "Alice is simply helping with another simulation."

Though she clearly didn't believe him, Jessamine was forced to turn the camera onto him and ask: "What do you mean?"

"One of the main reasons that we are put through the simulators so often before we go into space," said Karl smoothly, "is to completely familiarize us with the equipment. To keep us on our toes and to help us to cope in emergencies, the simulators are set up with a number of fake emergencies. This enables us to work out ways of combating problems in space and helps us to think on our feet. Or, in Alice's case, on her seat."

Lanie winced at Karl's terrible pun. She knew

that he was covering for Alice, of course, but it sounded good even to her ears. While the camera was focused on him, she was free to take a look at the lock. It had clearly been tampered with; one of the small bolts was sawn almost through. When Alice had closed the door, the bolt had parted and blocked the lock. Simple but effective—and undoubtedly Suki's handiwork again.

"So," Jessamine said, unconvinced, "this is just a test of what you'd do if you ever got locked in the lavatory?"

"Right," Karl agreed with a winning smile. "Those sorts of accidents do happen. Now, Alice could just bang on the door until one of us came along, or she could put her mind to it and improvise a way out." He hoped that Alice was getting his hint.

Calmed down now, Alice had indeed realized what he was saying. Time to stop and think her way out of this instead of getting all flustered. She heard a whisper—Lanie's voice. "Bolt sawn through, jamming lock."

Alice bent to examine the lock. Yes, she could see a bit of gleaming metal there. It blocked the return of the lock, so . . . the only thing to do was to take the lock apart. But with what?

Grinning, she pulled a stud off the uniform coverall that she and the rest of the group had been given. Using this as a screwdriver, she managed to slowly undo the lock. After a moment, it fell apart in her hands and the door swung open.

"And there we are," Karl said smoothly, as if he had had no doubts at all in his mind. "Another

73

problem solved, in the tradition of NASA."

"Very impressive," Jessamine said and headed off with Al to another training event.

Lanie let out a sigh of relief. "That was a close one. Another foul-up could have canned us." She grinned ruefully at her own pun. "Suki strikes again."

Alice nodded, and placed the pieces of the lock on the floor by the door. "Better make a note to get this fixed." She turned to her friends. "Thanks, guys. I almost blew it there."

Karl shrugged. "We're here to help one another, after all. Besides, we can't blame you for getting embarrassed."

Maybe he couldn't, but Alice could blame herself. For the rest of that day, she was completely lost in her own thoughts. The others—if they noticed it— said nothing to her. Alice was questioning her place on the team once again, and feeling very inadequate.

That night she couldn't sleep. She slipped out of bed and padded quietly to the window. They always slept with it open despite the heat, and the starlight streamed in. Staring out, she could see the northern stars here—many of them different from those of her home. But they still burned brightly, diamonds in the dark sky, calling to her.

"I couldn't sleep, either," Noemi said, softly. "I had to see the stars. Just think—soon we'll be out there, among them!"

"Maybe," Alice sighed. "If we don't screw up this film."

"Why should we?" Noemi demanded. "We've got

the best team there is. Nathan is a good leader; Karl is an excellent pilot; Gen is a whiz with the mechanics; Lanie can make those computers do anything she wants them to; and—"

"And I'm useless," Alice interrupted. "I nearly lost my cool today and blew the whole thing for us."

In sudden understanding, Noemi looked surprised. "But any of us might have had a moment like that. I can hardly believe that you, of all people, should feel this way."

"Me of all people?" Alice laughed bitterly. "And what do I contribute to the group? I'm lucky to even be on this course. I should be back home, on the farm, where I belong."

"No," Noemi told her firmly. "You are where you should be. You do not belong on a farm. There is no shame in being a farmer. Many people in my own Venezuela are farmers. But it is right only if one wishes to be one. You have the stars in your eyes and heart. If you were to return to your farm, you would regret it for the rest of your life. Your farm would grow hateful to you.

"And, besides that, you're a real member of the team. You bring your farming skills. We'll need your talents on Mars, to grow the crops to stay alive. And your level head and calm understanding help us through tough spots. You may not be the best pilot, or the fastest on the computer—but so what? You offer us so much. Without you, our team would be much weaker."

Alice was warmed by her friend's words. "You really think so?" she asked.

"I know so," Noemi assured her. "You would

make a grave mistake if you didn't stay with us." She laughed. "I am, of course, speaking very selfishly. If you don't stay on the team, I don't think we'll be able to survive on Mars. And then I'd be very unhappy myself. So, to please me, if for no other reason, stick it out."

Alice thought about it for a moment. Perhaps Noemi was right. She certainly *wanted* to go to Mars. "Okay," she promised. "I'm going to stick it out."

"Terrific," Noemi smiled. "Now, let's get some rest, okay?"

As if to underline Alice's decision to stay on the project, she received a letter a few days later. It was from a fifth-grade student in Ohio, and Alice read through it twice.

"Dear Miss Thorne," it began. "You don't know me. I'm a student who has been given a report to do on role models. I would like to know something about you to use in my report. I feel close to you because I also live on a farm and want to be an astronaut. Please write soon. Sincerely, Tammi Jensen."

A role model, Alice thought. Me! It was a heavy responsibility to bear, but she remembered what her mom had told her. She was showing others that there was a way for them to follow. Tammi Jensen was one of them. Maybe in eight years, Tammi would be on another program like this, training for

. . . where? Mars? The moons of Jupiter? Icarus station? Alice felt suddenly proud and privileged to be on the To Mars Together project. She was only one of the first among many, and she was setting an example for the ones to come. It was important that it be a good example.

Picking up her pen and a sheet of paper, she began to compose a letter back to Tammi encouraging the next generation of pioneers . . .

Chapter Ten

"So . . ." Jessamine asked, as Al panned the camera about the girls' room, "what do you girls do in your spare time?"

"Spare time?" Noemi asked. "What's that?"

"We don't have a lot of free hours," Alice said quickly. "Especially now that we're getting closer to the lift-off date. We have to do simulator work, field trips, and take regular classes in some very irregular subjects like geology, plumbing, and auto mechanics. Then, in the evenings, we're expected to read. We've got a list that's several hundred books long, as well as dozens of magazine articles. Then, when we can, we have to fit in gym classes to stay in shape."

"But you must get some time off," Jessamine persisted. "What do you do then?"

"I *shop*," Noemi answered cheerily. She flung open the door of the small closet that had been allocated to her. It was packed with her huge selection of fashion outfits. Never one to be tidy, Noemi had crammed clothing, shoes, bags, and hats in anywhere she could. It looked ready to explode all over the room.

"What are you going to do with them?" the reporter asked in amazement.

"Wear as many as possible."

"No, I mean when you go to Mars. Isn't there a limit to the amount of personal stuff you can take?"

The smile on Noemi's face froze abruptly as the implications of what Jessamine had said sank in.

Not only would there be nowhere to shop on Mars—there wouldn't even be room for what she'd already bought. And she hadn't even worn half of the clothes yet . . .

As if oblivious to the change in Noemi's mood, Jessamine continued. "What do they pay you people anyway? It must be a fortune if you can buy all of those clothes."

"Oh, no," Alice broke in. "We don't get paid. If we choose to return, we will receive a scholarship for college. Right now, all our needs are taken care of at the center."

"Then how can she afford so many clothes?"

"Her father pays for them."

Jessamine started playing about with her small computer. "Ah . . . I see that her father is an industrialist, and a very wealthy one at that. It makes sense she'd get on the program. Her father's 'donation' probably took care of that."

"That's not true!" The comments about her father had finally snapped Noemi out of her thoughts. "My father would never pay for me to come on this course. I *earned* the right. Stop saying whatever filthy lies you dream up, especially about my family!"

Jessamine stopped filming, but she still looked very pleased with herself. "I think we've gotten some very interesting footage here," she observed. "Thank you." She and Al left.

Lanie grabbed Noemi's arm to prevent the furious girl from following. "Chill out!" she hissed. "Can't you see that she's just trying to get a reaction out of you? Don't give her the satisfaction."

Noemi nodded reluctantly and Lanie let her go. Still angry, Noemi kicked at a pile of clothes on the floor. It sailed across the room.

"Pick it up," Alice said. "Let's keep the place tidy."

"Who appointed you mother?" Noemi yelled furiously. "If you want it picked up, pick it up yourself." She grabbed her bag and stormed out of the room.

Lanie raised an eyebrow. "Boy, she's really buzzing. I'll go along and keep an eye on her. The mood she's in, she'll wreck that pretty car of hers."

"It'd just give her an excuse to buy another," Alice sighed as Lanie dashed off down the corridor. Wearily, Alice closed the door, and looked at the top on the floor. "Well, I guess I'd better pick it up myself."

Wincing as the Mercedes screeched down the road to Houston, Lanie tried to pretend that she wasn't cowering in her seat. "So . . ." she said lightly, "where are we going?"

"Where the tough go when the going gets rough."

"Ah," Lanie sighed. "Shopping."

"Right."

After a few minutes of Noemi's crazy driving, Lanie discovered that it was much easier to endure if she closed her eyes and prayed. Finally, though, the trip was over, and Noemi slammed her car to a halt in a parking space that Lanie would have bet was two feet too small for the car. She had to be very careful getting out that she didn't open her door another inch and drive a deep gash down the Toyota in the next spot.

Inside the mall, Noemi seemed to be just as manic. She stormed into the first clothing shop she could find and started slamming her way through the closest rack. It was filled with sequined tops that glittered as Lanie whirled through them.

"Are we looking for anything in particular?" Lanie asked, somewhat nervously. She had never seen Noemi in a mood like this. "Or just browsing?"

Noemi slammed her hand onto the rack, and strode across to the next one. It was of knee-length pants. Again, she flicked through them as if they were invisible to her. By now, Lanie was getting worried. She'd been on enough shopping sprees with her friend to know that Noemi had normally pulled at least three outfits to try on by this point. "You feeling okay?" she asked.

"No," answered Noemi in a very small voice. Then, abruptly, she sat down on the floor, buried her face in her hands, and started to sob.

Great, thought Lanie. *This is just what I needed.*

Chapter Eleven

Noemi sat in a huddle on the floor by the T-shirt rack, crying softly to herself. Feeling somewhat uncomfortable, Lanie glanced around the shop. One of the young sales assistants, with frizzed hair and far too much makeup was staring at them as if they were roaches crawling out of her lunch. Lanie waved the girl away and sat down on the floor next to her friend.

"Hey, come on," she said encouragingly. "What's wrong?"

"Everything," Noemi managed to get out between sobs.

"Yeah, well, can you get more specific?"

Turning her tear-stained face up, Noemi nodded. Catching her breath, she managed: "I *hate* that Jarvis woman!"

"You're not the only one," observed Lanie, dryly.

"Why does she always have to be so . . . so . . . mean?"

Lanie shrugged. "Some people are like that.

Maybe she feels she's doing a service to the public, prying out hidden secrets. And making them up when there's nothing hidden. Maybe she just doesn't like space travel. Maybe she just enjoys annoying people happier than she is. Who knows?"

Noemi sniffed, then dabbed at her eyes with a wad of tissues. "It's so depressing."

"What? That there are people happier than she is?"

"No." Waving a hand all around, Noemi explained. "All of this."

"I don't get it," Lanie admitted. "I thought you loved all of this."

"I do. That's why it's so depressing." Noemi blew her nose. "That woman made me realize that it's all so pointless. It doesn't matter what I buy, I can't take it with me. It's got stay on Earth when we lift off. So what's the point of buying anything?" She looked so miserable that Lanie reached out and hugged her. It seemed to help. Noemi blew her nose again, and continued. "What's even worse is that I just realized something. We have a weight restriction that will apply to clothes. I can't take along many changes. *What are we going to wear on Mars for the next three years?* Those monotonous red overalls? I don't think I could stand it."

Shaking herself free, Lanie replied. "Well, I, doubt it'll be that bad. There's always the space suits." Her attempt at humor fell flat so she carried on. "I'm sure we'll be allowed to take some special things. Look at it as a challenge. You can be the fashion trend-setter for Mars. And just think of all the fun you'll have checking out the new Earth fashions three years from now."

"You're just trying to make me feel better," Noemi protested, a hint of a smile finally emerging.

"Yeah, well, that *is* the general idea," Lanie admitted. "But it's true. Use your imagination, and whatever we take with us. Start some new trends. Hey, we'll be in the news often enough — maybe what you do will catch on. It's worth a try at least, isn't it?"

Noemi nodded. "I guess so." She stood up again, and reached in her bag for her mirror. "Ugh, I look awful."

"That'll teach you to sit on the floor and cry in public."

Blushing, Noemi suddenly looked around and realized what she had been up to. The freaky-looking sales assistant gave her a cold stare. Noemi felt two inches tall. "Let's get out of here," she muttered. Grinning, Lanie led the way.

Out among the other shoppers, she steered Noemi toward the ice-cream stall. "Best cure for depression I know. You'll never see anyone eating ice cream and looking unhappy at the same time." She ordered two large soft chocolate cones with sprinkles and they wandered through the mall, licking and looking in the store windows.

"How come you never buy new clothes?" Noemi asked suddenly.

Pausing in midlick, Lanie shrugged. "I know I dress lousy. I just like this old jacket of mine. It's comfortable."

"I'm not criticizing," said Noemi. "I'm just curious."

"Habit, I guess," the other girl answered, catching a trickle of ice slush on her tongue before it could fall to the floor. "My mother could never spare any money to buy me nice things. She spent it all on booze. She never cared what I wore. So I never really got too bothered about clothes."

"Except that leather jacket."

"Yeah." Lanie looked down, her face turning slightly pink. "It's just about the only thing my mom ever bought for me. She'd been on a real binge one time and started crying about how much she loved me, and how she never got me anything. Normally she'd go through that kind of thing once a month or so, and get it out of her system before she got stoned again. This time, I guess it stuck in her mind the next day, despite her hangover. She came back that night with this jacket for me. And a couple of bottles for herself. I was ten at the time."

After a moment, Noemi said, in a small voice, "You know, we're a lot alike, Lanie."

"Yeah, right!" Lanie snorted, good-naturedly. "Me, I'm from a ghetto, with just what I stand up in, and a mom who wouldn't recognize me unless she saw me through the bottom of a whiskey bottle. You—you're from a different world."

Noemi shook her head. "Not that different. Oh, sure, I have two parents, and a lot of clothes, and money to throw away if I want. But so what? I can't really talk to my mother. She's always running around to another party or a reception, or to play at the tennis club. I don't remember when I said more than a few words to her. And my father . . . well, he's a nice man, but I don't think he actually even misses me. I was just another expense he always paid. He was always looking for me to get married to some well-connected young man—like a business merger, I guess." She fished in her bag for her wad of credit cards. "You know why I started to use these? For him to notice me. I figured he'd get good and mad and yell at me or something, just to show that what I did mattered to him. You know what he did? He paid every single bill without a word."

Lanie shrugged again. "Maybe that's his idea of love, Noemi. Maybe he doesn't know any other way. I'm not exactly an expert in the field of fathers. I never knew mine. I couldn't even tell you his name. Mom couldn't even remember it."

Tears started to fill Noemi's eyes again. "All I ever wanted from my father was just some attention. And all he ever gave me was *money*. You know, when I was top of my classes in anything, he never said a word. And when I was accepted on this course, you know what he said?" When Lanie shook her head, Noemi replied: "He said: 'I expect this means that there'll be no wedding for you for a while.' And that was it. No congratulations, no 'I'm so proud of you,' not even 'I forbid you to go.' *Nothing*. I wish I knew what he wanted from me."

"Maybe he doesn't want anything," Lanie suggested. "Maybe he's happy with whatever you are, or want to be?"

"Well, *I'm* not," retorted Noemi. "I want to have some purpose to my life, some meaning. That's why I applied for this Mars Project. To be part of something worthwhile."

"And you are. Alice, Nathan, me, and the rest. We like you, and we need you for our team." She held up a hand to stop Noemi saying anything. "Hey, don't get me wrong! I don't like finding your clothes all over the floor, or your two tons of makeup crowding out the bathroom. But, despite all of that, you're an okay person, and you really are a good member of the team. I don't care if your father needs you or not. *We* need you." She paused and smiled. "You are like me, all right — we both found ourselves a real place to stay at last, and people who care about us." She looked hard at Noemi, and then grimaced. "Boy, I sound like a bad soap opera. Let's knock it off before I start crying, too."

88

Noemi smiled, and used her tissues to wipe away the last of her tears. "Okay. Anyway, I've got two things I really have to do. First . . ." She walked back into the clothing store that they had recently left, Lanie trailing behind. To the weird sales girl, she asked, "Do you have a pair of scissors?"

Glaring slightly, the girl fished under the cash register and produced a large pair. Noemi thanked her, and then took out her pile of credit cards. She jerked one out and cut it into several pieces. Lanie caught on, and picked up a bin. Noemi smiled her thanks and dumped the shredded card into it. Then she started on the next card.

"Hey!" the salesgirl said, taken aback. "What are you doing?"

"I don't need these anymore," Noemi told her, happily. "I'm going to Mars."

The girl looked at her, worried. "Whatever you say, honey," Lanie could see that she was wondering if she should call the police and report a nutcase on the loose.

Noemi finished her butchery on the cards and handed the scissors back to the girl. "Thank you so much." Then, still grinning, she linked her arm through Lanie's and marched her out into the mall again.

"What's that one for?" Lanie asked when she saw Noemi put one last credit card in her pocket.

Grinning, Noemi replied, "Emergencies. I may

be a reformed shopaholic, but I'm not *stupid*."

"And what's the second thing you've got to do?" Lanie asked, puzzled.

"I've got to clean up my room."

Chapter Twelve

Nathan wiped the sweat away from his forehead with the back of his sleeve and bent down to the chassis of the Martian Rover again. Parts from the transmission were scattered about him and Karl as they worked to discover what had failed them. They were supposed to be testing out the Rover, one of the vehicles they would assemble and use on Mars. As part of their training, each of the groups had been given a list of parts and free access to the supply rooms. They were then told to get a Rover operational.

There had been no problem in putting the vehicle together. When it was all assembled, however, it simply didn't run. So the team had been forced to start stripping it down, to try to discover where the problem lay. It was a long, tedious task, and it was not helped by the fact that Gen simply hadn't shown up for this session.

This was hardly anything new for the Japanese boy. He skipped classes from time to time, since he could always catch up with no trouble. But he didn't normally miss the practicals, and this was one time they could really have used his help.

Nathan cursed quietly to himself as he used a wrench to take out the obstinate nut he was working on. Oil splattered him, and he swore louder. Then he twisted the wrench too sharply. It spun in his fingers, and, slippery with the oil, he lost his grip. The tool slammed across his knuckles as it fell, skinning them badly. He swore for the third time, and pulled back his hand.

Seeing the blood across his knuckles, Alice grabbed him and hauled him out. "You'd better wash that hand immediately," she told him. "It could get infected if you don't." When he started to protest, she glared at him. "Go!"

He went.

Karl snickered to himself. "Poor Nathan," he called out. "Mommy won't let him play."

"Watch it," Sergei joked. "She may hit you with the wrench next!" He slipped under the Rover to join Karl and began working on the loosened nut. Pointedly ignoring the two boys, Alice rejoined Lanie and Noemi at the table where they were testing the electrical systems from the Rover.

Lanie threw down her screwdriver in disgust. "It all checks out," she said. "Nothing wrong here that I can see. I don't know why it isn't working."

"What we really need," Alice sighed, "is Gen. He'd probably be able to spot the trouble in a second."

"Yeah," growled Lanie. "Only he can't be bothered to show up. You'd think he didn't want to be a part of the team."

Noemi eyed the jumble of wiring and the screwdriver. Then she looked at her nails. It would be almost inevitable that she'd break one if she helped out. "Why don't I go and look for him?" she suggested. "I'm not really too good with this sort of problem so you wouldn't miss me."

"What you really mean," groused Lanie, "is that you're afraid you'll break a nail."

To avoid any argument, Alice broke in. "That's probably a good idea, Noemi. Thank you."

Gen wasn't in his room when Noemi knocked. She tried the door, and it was unlocked. The room was empty, and she noticed that Gen's guitar was gone from its usual spot at the bottom of his bed. He was obviously off practicing it, and had probably lost track of the time.

She knew that Karl and Sergei had forbidden Gen to practice in their room. Gen was into heavy metal, and it was impossible to concentrate on anything while he was playing. That was fine for him, since he only had to read a page once to memorize it, but for the others it was sheer hell.

The only answer had been for him to play in the basement. That way, Karl had remarked rather cruelly, only the rats would be annoyed. She rushed off down the stairs and could hear the strains of his guitar even through the thick fire doors.

Closer in, it was almost deafening. Steeling her nerves, she managed to peer around the door to the little supply room that Gen had taken over. He was playing away at full steam, eyes closed, and his face twisted into a huge grin. Slamming his hand across the electric guitar's strings, he dragged the most horrendous noise from it.

She tried to call to him, but there was simply no chance he'd be able to hear her. Instead, she walked over, and pulled the plug on his guitar.

Gen slapped the strings again, and jumped in surprise when there was no sound. His eyes flashed open, and he jumped again when he saw Noemi watching him. Then he realized what she'd done. He moved to plug the instrument back in again, but she grabbed his arm.

"We had a practical at two," she reminded him. "Did you forget?"

"I *never* forget," he told her. "Hey, don't be so uptight," he added. "It's no big deal. I'll catch up next time. I'm on a roll here." He tried once more to replug the guitar, and she stopped him again.

"It's a team effort," she said. "We need your help. The Rover isn't working."

"Man," he sighed. Then he shrugged and slipped out of the guitar strap. "Well, I guess it's up to me to save your butts again."

Noemi scowled. "That's no attitude to take."

"Hey, cool it. I'll do it. Someone's got to do the work, after all."

"Meaning?" she asked darkly.

He gestured at her clothes. "I don't see any grease spots on you."

"I was helping with the wiring," she said coldly.

"Right." He started off up the stairs. "And I'm a

94

Teenage Mutant Ninja Turtle."

They argued all the way back to the laboratory area where the rest of the group was still struggling with the Rover. It lay there in a few more pieces now but was still clearly not on the road to being repaired. Alice was gently but firmly bandaging up Nathan's hand.

"I hear you need help," Gen grinned, ambling across to the broken-down vehicle. He bent to take a look, and then pointed. "You've put in the wrong plugs. You want the next size down. Can't you guys even read a chart right without me to hold your hands?"

Karl straightened up, glaring. "It's so kind of you to condescend to help us."

Gen shrugged. "Hey, no sweat. But you should be more careful. I may not be around to save your butts on Mars all the time."

Getting to his feet, Karl said, "It seems to me that you're not around very much at all when you should be."

"Hey, I pass all the courses, and I save your hides for you. I'm entitled to a little personal freedom."

"You're supposed to be working *with* us, not for us," Sergei broke in, just as annoyed as Karl. "If you had been here when you were supposed to have been, then we might have put this Rover together properly the first time."

"I guess," said Gen casually. "I'd never have let you make such a dumb mistake." He started to walk away. Karl grabbed his shirt.

"Where are you going?"

Gen shrugged free of his grip. "I've done what you wanted and solved the problem. Now I'm going back to my music."

"You are scheduled to be with this group for the rest of the afternoon."

"Tough." Gen started to move away again. "I know this thing backward already. I don't need to waste my time."

"*You* may think it's a waste of time," Karl snapped. "But the rest of us think otherwise."

"Then the rest of you stay." He glared at the hand that Karl laid on him. "Let go of me."

Nathan moved smoothly between them. "Hey, knock it off, guys," he said. "There's no need for this." Turning to Gen, he added, "Karl is right. You *are* supposed to be with us. We're supposed to be a team."

"Sure," Gen agreed, lazily. "And we are. But this team member has learned his lessons already, and wants to go out and play. Is that okay, *Daddy?*"

"No, it isn't. You're down to help, and you'll stay and help. Like the rest of us do."

"Oh? You want me to screw up, too—?"

"I'll tell you what I want you to do," Karl broke in. "And where I'd like you to go. I'll even provide you with a road map on how to get there."

Lanie pushed in to help Nathan. "Come on, guys," she said. "Let's knock off this macho crap and get on with the work, okay? We want to pass this class and go on to Mars, don't we?"

Reluctantly, both Karl and Gen nodded, and the

Rover began slowly to take shape again. This time, though, once it was assembled, the motor purred. Everyone but Karl and Gen had grinned at that point.

Dr. Thompson had come around to check on their progress. Seeing the Rover being put through its paces by Karl and Alice, he had made some notes and left. Clearly, this was another of the tests they had passed. If they hadn't, he would have had something to say to them.

Over dinner that night, the mood was still pretty tense between Karl and Gen. Karl was still toying with his food, after Gen bolted his own down.

"The best way to eat it," Noemi said, "is to do it without tasting it."

"I have a theory," Lanie offered. "I figure that NASA knows we'll have some pretty poor meals to start with on Mars till we grow our own supplies. So, to make that food look good, they're serving up this pig slop here. After this, *anything* is bound to taste good."

Gen finished his plate, and left them, all without a word. Nathan stared at his retreating back. "I think we have a problem."

"Yes," said Karl. "Gen."

"Let's face it, guys," Lanie broke in. "He doesn't really need us along. That memory of his makes everything we do seem so simple to him. He's probably just bored."

"It makes sense," Nathan agreed. "But his boredom may well cost the team its place. He has to learn to fit in with us and work with us—not off on his own."

"And how do you propose we fix it?" asked Sergie. He had been reading a letter from one of his girlfriends, Ludmilla. It didn't seem to have pleased him, but he finally dragged himself away from it joined in with the discussion.

"Perhaps I should beat some sense into him," Karl suggested.

Nathan wasn't absolutely certain this was a joke. "I think we need something more constructive than that. He has to be made to see that he is a member of this team. As such, he's got to pull his weight."

"Somehow," Lanie remarked dryly, "I doubt that an appeal to logic will do much good. He's too impulsive for that."

"So now what?" Nathan asked. No one had any suggestions to make at all.

Chapter Thirteen

The next day Gen was present at the first class of the day, when Dr. Thompson handed out their afternoon assignments. Nathan and his team were each given a five-page printout.

"Space welding," Sergei grunted. "Well, that should be interesting."

"And useful," Alice agreed. "Considering the fact that we have to help assemble the Mars ships in orbit."

Gen scanned his sheets and then threw them aside. "Big deal," he said. "It's all computerized anyway. Should be simple to get the hang of." He closed his eyes and lay back in his chair. Clearly his uncooperative mood from the day before wasn't over yet.

The other groups had different assignments, and Dr. Thompson spent time with each group, going over what they would have to do before crossing to join Nathan and his team. Gen snapped alert for this part.

"Right," their adviser told them. "You'll all meet

in the test lab at two o'clock. You'll all get your chance to try the laser techniques, but be very certain you understand the control procedures. That laser can be very dangerous if it isn't handled properly."

"We'll be careful," Nathan promised.

Dr. Thompson nodded. "Good. I've persuaded Miss Jarvis to film another group this afternoon. I don't want any of you nervous with this equipment."

He moved off to the next group, and Gen yawned very deliberately. "Well, you dudes had better start your studying. We don't want any mistakes, you know." He stood up. "Catch you later."

"Where do you think you're going?" Nathan asked, annoyed.

"Wherever I please, leader-man. I already know my part." He tossed off a mock salute and left the room.

Nathan was furious but still not sure how to handle Gen. His cocky attitude was dragging down the morale of the rest of the team. Nathan's first job was to get them working together again. "Right," he sighed. "Let's make sure we know what we're doing, crew." He ruffled his handout. "We'd better check the whole thing through."

Together, they started to work over the papers. They detailed the computer codes and paths to be used to program the laser welder mock-up. After a while, though, Lanie frowned.

"This isn't right," she finally said. "These figures

are wrong."

"Are you sure?" Nathan asked.

"This is my field," Lanie assured him. "I *know* there's a mistake here." She did a quick calculation in her head. "Yeah, they've accidentally switched these two figures around."

Karl had been following her calculations, and nodded. "She's right," he agreed. "And that makes almost all of this printout wrong."

"We'd better tell Dr. Thompson," Nathan decided.

To his surprise, the astronaut didn't seem disturbed when they told him of the error. "Fine," he said. "You'd better make the corrections then."

Lanie glared at him. "You knew there was a mistake."

He grinned back at them. "Of course. It was another test. Like I said, this is dangerous equipment you're using. We had to be certain you really did know what you were doing. If you hadn't caught that mistake, I'd never have let you on the laser."

As they wandered back to their desks, Sergei shook his head in wonder. "They don't miss a trick, do they?"

"Let's hope that *we* don't," Noemi answered.

They worked on the papers, correcting the small errors that had been introduced. When they were certain that they had them correct, they showed them to Dr. Thompson. He scanned the calculations, and then handed them back.

"Good work," he approved. "I'll see you at two then."

"We'd better make a copy for Gen," Nathan sighed, as they were leaving. "Otherwise there might be trouble."

"I'd like to give him trouble," Sergei scowled. "He should be here with us, not off fooling about with that annoying music of his."

"I'll do it," Alice offered. "I'll give him the papers when he decides to turn up."

Gen finally showed up with barely a minute to spare. The rest of the group had been waiting outside the test lab, their tempers growing thinner all of the time. Gen sauntered up, his hands in his pockets, a silly grin on his face.

"Awesome," he said in mock horror. "Look at the faces on you guys."

"Well, you should have been working with us this morning . . ." Nathan began.

"Don't lecture me," Gen begged. "I don't want to hear it. Stay cool, dude."

Alice held out the corrected papers. "You'd better take a look at these," she told him. Gen took them, and was about to say something when the lab door opened and Dr. Thompson looked out.

"Good. Okay, let's get started."

They filed into the small room and looked about. Opposite the door was a large glass screen separating them from the actual laser. Below the screen was the control console. In the other room, the laser was mounted on a mock-up of the shuttle arm. In space, the armature would move the laser into position for the welding. Here, the controls would move the mock-up so they could all get used to the process.

"The other room is in a vacuum," Dr. Thompson told them. "That way, you'll be able to work in the right conditions. But be very careful. If the laser beam accidentally hits this window, then the glass will shatter. There'd be a pretty bad explosion of air out of here into the other room and it could seriously injure all of you. So keep that beam on the right path."

Three of them would work the process at any one time. Two of them were using remote manipulators to hold the two pieces of metal in place while the third person used the laser to weld them together. The manipulators were fun to play with, like the power gloves used in some video games. They were bulky gloves with electronic sensors in them, connected to robot hands in the other room. Once one of the team donned a pair of the gloves, anything that they did with their hands was fed through the computer and to the two sets of mechanical claws in the other room.

Nathan and Alice took the first turn with the manipulators. These were mounted on the console to keep them steady, and they simply thrust their own hands into them. Nathan flexed his hands in the gloves and saw the spidery claws in the other room copy his actions. He grinned, and drummed his fingers. The hand tapped its own fingers on the floor. Alice laughed, and copied his actions. Her own claws did the same in the other room.

Then they started to work. Nathan made the claws grasp a sheet of aluminum. He lifted it up and brought it toward the laser. Alice brought a second piece, and they carefully positioned the two. "Ready," Nathan told Karl, who was taking the first run with the laser.

Karl nodded, and keyed in the codes for the beam. When he was happy with the settings, he turned on the power.

Despite what they had all seen in films, the laser didn't emit any visible light. Instead, where the two pieces of aluminum were being held together, a line of bright red started to appear as the metal melted and flowed together. Using the controls, Karl carefully ran the beam down the length of the join. The metal started to cool behind the path, and they could all see that Karl was managing a pretty decent straight line. Finally, reaching the end of the sheets, he snapped off the beam. After a moment, the red glow of hot metal cooled.

Dr. Thompson nodded. "Pretty good work, Karl," he approved. "You're a natural at this."

"Practice," the boy admitted. "I've used regular welding equipment before. This isn't that different."

"Different enough," the doctor commented. "Okay, switch places."

This time Lanie and Noemi took the gloves,

and Gen moved to the computer controls. Lanie quickly used the glove to give Gen a rude gesture from the claw inside the room. He didn't care, and simply grinned away. As Lanie and Noemi got the hang of moving the claws, Gen flicked through the program for the laser and then sighed rather loudly. "Come on, dudes," he said. "Let's get this show on the road."

Angry at her teammate, Lanie brought her sheet of metal together with Noemi's with a squeal from both sheets that set everyone's teeth on edge. Gen simply switched on the power.

The laser beam hit the edge of the sheet of aluminum instead of the joint and it started to spray molten globs across the floor. Frowning, Gen frantically keyed the controls again. Instead of the laser moving into the correct position to start the line of welding, though, the arm it was on began to spin about.

The laser began to move toward the glass screen separating the two rooms.

Remembering Dr. Thompson's warning, Gen frantically tapped in further instructions to return the laser to its original position. Instead, the beam hit the wall, just inches from the glass. Gen froze in horror as the beam tracked toward them.

Karl shouldered him aside quickly and worked fast to key in fresh instructions. The beam suddenly cut out, and then the armature returned to the rest position.

They were safe.

Dr. Thompson turned angrily on Gen. "What the hell were you doing? Didn't you pay any attention to what I said?"

"But . . . but . . ." Gen appeared to be utterly confused. "I did it the way it was on the sheet!" he cried. "I *know* I did."

"But that was all wrong," Lanie snapped. "Didn't you read the revisions that we gave you?"

Gen looked down at the floor, burning in shame. "I . . . I thought it was the same handout. I didn't even look at it."

Finally, Dr. Thompson caught on. "Wait a minute," he said coldly. "Do you mean that you weren't there when your teammates worked out the problems this morning?"

Gen shook his head, not daring to look up. "I just memorized the sheet. I didn't know that it was wrong."

Dr. Thompson scowled down at the crimson-faced boy. "I trust this will be a lesson to you. I don't want it to happen again."

"It won't," Gen promised very quietly. "I'm sorry."

Nodding curtly, Dr. Thompson turned back to the others. "Right, let's carry on with the practice. Who's next?"

That evening, Gen came to Nathan, looking very sheepish. "I just want to apologize," he said. "I behaved very badly."

"Yeah, you did," Nathan agreed, pulling no punches.

"If I ever start getting swell-headed again, just remind me about it, okay?"

Nathan grinned. "With your photographic memory? No way you'll need reminding. Right, teammate?" He stuck out his hand.

"Totally," Gen agreed, shaking happily.

Chapter Fourteen

Nathan had remained puzzled by the strange hatred that Suki Long seemed to bear for him and his group. Nothing they had ever done had given her cause for this. She had never made it clear why she tried so hard to make certain that Nathan's group failed. He was at a loss to understand her attitude.

He had actually asked her about it directly at one point. All of the students took a set number of classes a week together, since they all had to learn many of the same skills. One was on celestial navigation — vital for them to study for their trip to Mars. The instructor was explaining the basics of using the stars as reference points when Gen, who knew this backward, got bored and leaned over to talk behind his hand to Sergei. Nathan had caught a glimpse of movement and saw that Suki had reached over to change some of Gen's calculations.

Nathan didn't want to make a scene in the class. Instead of saying anything, he threw a wadded-up ball of paper at her. It hit Suki's hand, and she whipped around guiltily, her face turning red as she realized she'd been spotted. But she was not the only one.

"Mr. Long," the lecturer said. "I had assumed that you were old enough not to need to pass love letters to your girlfriends in class. I would appreciate it if the two of you arranged your romantic assignations outside of the lecture theater."

It was Nathan's turn to be violently embarrassed. Even Alice laughed along with everyone else. Nathan looked down at his notes quickly, and the lecture went on.

After the class, he grabbed Suki's arm before she could leave. "I want to talk to you," he told her.

A group of the other kids, seeing him, mistook his motives. "Hey, Long," one guy called, "remember the curfew if you're dating!"

Nathan ignored them and concentrated on Suki. She looked bored rather than guilty. "I saw what you were doing—trying to get Gen into trouble."

"So sue me," she snapped.

"I don't get it," Nathan said. "Why are you always trying to get us bumped? You're doing fine. You're definitely on the Mars mission. So why won't you just cooperate with everyone? We've all got to start working together on this."

She looked at him in something like disgust. "Sickening," she replied. "Just the sort of wimpy talk I'd expect from you. All in this together! That's a laugh! Mister High and Mighty American, condescending to let the backward nations in on the crumbs from your cakes!"

"What's with you?" Nathan asked her. "How come you've got this chip on your shoulder?"

"This isn't a world where people make friends, Long! Get real—it's a jungle. Survival of the fittest. The rules of life are the rules of the jungle—anything you can do to win is fair. That's what I live by. And it'll be the same on Mars. Only the strong will survive."

Nathan looked at her in pity. "I feel sorry for you, Suki. You're missing the point of the whole project." He turned his back on her and started to walk away.

"I don't need your pity, Long!" she yelled after him. "I don't need *anything* you have!"

Spinning, he snapped back, "Yes you do. I don't know why, but you need that first place on the mission. And you won't get it, because our team is the best." He could see that this had hit home hard with her. She clenched her teeth, controlling her temper with great difficulty.

"I shall get it," she snarled. "Whatever it may take."

Over the next few weeks, she tried several more times to sabotage their efforts. Thankfully, one or other of the team was always on the alert for this, and they managed to prevent any further incidents.

Nathan had been doing a little extra study work on the computers one evening, worried about falling behind. Working away, he didn't realize that Jessamine Jarvis and Al were even in the room until they began to talk. They clearly didn't know he was still there, either, so he hunched down and stopped typing.

"I caught that Long kid going through my tapes," Al told his boss.

"What?" Jessamine looked furious. "Is he trying to get hold of those embarrassing bits? Another NASA cover-up?"

"No," Al said, patiently, "not the boy. The girl."

"Oh. *Her.*" After a moment's thought, Jessamine suggested, "Transfer all of the footage of the screw-ups onto one master tape, Al. And keep it on you all the time. I don't want to chance any of the kids getting hold of it and ruining it."

"Sure," replied Al agreeably. "But I don't get it. Why was she after the tapes?"

"Because you filmed her fouling up. Don't you know who she is?"

Al shrugged.

"And you call · yourself a reporter," Jessamine sniffed. "You should know about her. Her father is—"

At that moment, the door opened, and Dr. Thompson walked into the room. The two reporters stopped talking and looked at the adviser somewhat guiltily.

"Oh," Thompson said slowly. "I was looking for one of the students. Excuse me."

"I think we're alone here. Al and I were just leaving anyway."

After they were gone, Dr. Thompson turned and called out, "Long, get Miss Rizzo and meet me in my office in fifteen minutes." Then he left.

Nathan stood up, astonished. He had known that Nathan was there all along. Their instructor certainly had a few surprises up his sleeve.

Just how many, Nathan didn't discover until he and Lanie arrived in Thompson's office. Already waiting there was Suki, a smug smile on her face. On the desk was a sheaf of computer printouts.

Without looking up, Thompson called out, "Close the door." When they did so, he held out the top page to them. Lanie took one look at it and went white.

Nathan looked it over, and understood why. It was headed: Chicago Police Department

Underneath was the report of the arrest of Lanie Johnson — with a very clear picture of Lanie attached to it.

Chapter Fifteen

After a few minutes of shocked silence, Dr. Thompson cleared his throat. "There is more, of course," he informed them. Ruffling the pile of papers, he went on. "Falsified background for Lanie Rizzo, fake tests, reports . . . Miss Long brought all of this to me a short while ago. Now, Miss Rizzo, do you have anything to say?"

Lanie was shaking. She looked down at the papers and said miserably, "I guess it was bound to end sometime. I was just fooling myself."

"And a lot of other people, too, it would seem," Dr. Thompson observed. "Quite a lot of false information. I gather you admit that it is faked?"

"Yeah," Lanie whispered. "My name really is Lanie Johnson, and that was me that the cops arrested. But I didn't mean any harm by what I did. I just wanted out of the projects."

"Tell me all about how you managed this." He listened patiently as she explained how she had helped Cindy Rizzo with her work, and how they had built up a false background for "Lanie Rizzo" together. Finally, he interrupted her. "But *why* did you feel you had to lie about it?"

"Well," she said, angrily, at last, "would you even have read my application if I'd told you the truth?"

"Probably not," he admitted.

"I figured that. My only chance to get on this project was to fake it all. That's why I did it."

Dr. Thompson nodded almost sympathetically. Then he turned to stare at Nathan. "I notice that none of this seems to come as a surprise to you, Mr. Long. I take it that you knew, and helped her to cover it up—?"

"They *all* knew," Suki interrupted. "The whole team."

"Thank you," the adviser said firmly. "I will get to your story soon enough. Mr. Long?"

Hanging his head, Nathan nodded. "Yes, sir," he admitted. "We knew all about it. Karl discovered the truth and told us. We decided that the best thing to do was to hide the facts."

"Oh?" Dr. Thompson looked at them. "You took it on yourselves to carry on this . . . charade with her?"

"Yes, sir," said Nathan miserably.

"Well, I'm glad that you admit it." Thompson leaned back in his chair. "That's certainly a point in your favor, at least. So," he sighed, "what are we going to do about all of this?"

Lanie looked up, a fierce light burning in her eyes. "I guess you'll throw me out," she said. "I may as well go and pack right now. Just . . . well, don't blame Nathan and the rest. They were only doing what they thought was best."

"Really?"

"Yeah. They were trying to help me. It's not their fault, it's mine."

"So you take full responsibility for this deception then?"

Lanie shrugged. "I guess—"

"No, sir," Nathan broke in. "I'm the team leader. I was the one who convinced the others to go along with the cover-up."

"Ah." Dr. Thompson smiled briefly. "So now it's all your fault? Perhaps you'd care to come to some agreement as to who is to blame?"

Nathan couldn't understand this. Why was he putting them through this grilling? If he aimed to throw them off the course, why not just do it and be finished? Why all the playing around?

Shifting in his chair, Dr. Thompson indicated Suki. "Miss Long brought all of this information to my attention this afternoon," he told them. "She also suggested an intriguing solution to the whole problem." Suki looked very pleased with herself as he explained. "She proposes first that we eject Miss Rizzo from the course."

Hunched over, Lanie, almost in tears, said, "Yeah, well, I expected that."

"And secondly that we demote Mr. Long from team leader to the rank and file. To fill the missing place on the team and to act as new team leader, she proposes that she be appointed in his place."

Both Lanie and Nathan stared at Suki in horror. She wanted to take over their team!

"No way!" Nathan blurted out.

"You don't want to save the team?" Dr. Thompson asked him.

"Putting Suki in charge wouldn't save our team," Nathan explained. "It would ruin it. She couldn't fit in with us. She just wants to take over and give orders."

"So you oppose her solution?"

"Dead right I do. I think we'd sooner disband the team than have her in charge of it."

"Even if the alternative is all of you being rejected from the project?"

The bombshell had dropped, and Nathan's heart sank. All of their hopes and ambitions had come crashing down about them and Dr. Thompson was going to throw them all out.

"It wouldn't work," he said in despair. "Suki could never be a part of our team. She doesn't understand us, and she could never work with us. I'd sooner be thrown out."

"Don't be stupid!" Lanie cried. "There's no reason why the rest of you should suffer just for me. I'll take my lumps. Punish me, not all of them," she told Thompson.

"It's not just for you," Nathan argued. "It's for all of us. We're a team. We work together. I know none of the others would ever be able to accept Suki as a member of the team—let alone as leader."

"So you turn down the offer?" Dr. Thompson asked.

"Yeah," Nathan said, "we do." It felt like an execution—his and the others, along with Lanie. For the first time since he had met her, Lanie looked totally weak and vulnerable. She was on the verge of tears.

"Good. I'd have been worried if you had accepted it." Dr. Thompson picked up the papers and started

116

to tear them up.

"Wait a minute!" Suki snapped. "What are you doing?"

"What you should have done. Destroy these records."

"But . . . but . . ." Suki waved wildly at Lanie. "What about her? And the team? What are you going to do?"

"Give them twenty demerits," the supervisor said with a slight smile.

"And that's all?"

"That's all."

Neither Nathan nor Lanie could believe what they were hearing. They weren't being kicked off the project! Nor was the team being broken up! Hardly understanding, Lanie blurted out, "You're not gonna punish me?"

"You *have* to punish her," Suki insisted. "Otherwise you will be condoning her criminal behavior."

Clearly, Dr. Thompson had about reached his limit with Suki. "Shut up," he told her firmly. Startled, Suki did as she was told. "First of all, we're not condoning any of her behavior. Faking the computer records was stupid, but it wasn't criminal. Anyway, we've known all about that from day one."

"What?" Lanie couldn't believe her ears "You *knew* all along that it was faked?"

"Miss Rizzo," he said patiently, "we here at NASA have a very efficient computer staff. You're very good with your programming, but they've been working at it longer than you've even been alive. They red-flagged your data right from the start."

"So how come you took me?"

"Because we were interested. You showed a lot of skill with your work, and the test records were not faked. You proved that you had the ability to take our course here. Since you've been here, you've passed every test with ample margin, without faking. And the only time you broke into our computers was simply to look for information."

Lanie flushed with guilt. He even knew about her checking up on the team's record. She felt really stupid.

Dr. Thompson chuckled. "Actually, we gave you some extra points for that one," he admitted. "Ingenuity. So you see, we were never fooled by your attempts. On the other hand, there was never any reason to tell you what we knew so we kept it quiet."

"And her criminal record?" Suki insisted.

"That?" Dr. Thompson shrugged. "We all make mistakes — she just happened to be in the wrong place at the wrong time. We've had a careful eye on her while she's been here, and she's done nothing to suggest that she's less than honest. In fact, she's proven to be a lot more trustworthy than you have, Miss Long. I think that Miss Rizzo has learned her lessons from her past mistakes. I wish I could say the same for you."

Eyes spitting hate, Suki glared at the other youngsters, then back at the administrator. "I have copies of that file. I'm certain that Jessamine Jarvis would find them very interesting."

That was definitely the wrong thing to say. Dr. Thompson straightened up and answered very coldly. "I'm sure that she'd just love them, Miss Long. But I would strongly advise you not to let her see them.

118

Perhaps it's time that I made a few things clear to you." He stood up, towering over her slight figure. "I don't like you. You're mean-spirited, spiteful, nasty, and vindictive. You're exactly the wrong sort of person to be on this course. If it was up to me, you'd be thrown off so fast you'd get dizzy. But, as you well know, your father's influence on U.N. policies is pretty strong. Because of that, we're forced to tolerate you.

"However, if the news about Miss Rizzo was made known, Miss Jarvis might use it to try and wreck the entire project — or to severely embarrass us. If that were to happen, then we would feel that your father's goodwill would not be needed any longer. And neither would you. I trust I make myself clear? If that story comes out, then you will be on the next flight home. Understand?"

Slowly, reluctantly, Suki nodded. It took all of her self-control to do so, though.

"Good. Now I suggest that you go back to your room and think about what Alpha team has shown you concerning team spirit. They seem to be learning their lessons in helping one another pretty well."

Without another word, Suki spun about and stalked out of his office, slamming the door behind her. Dr. Thompson, looking relieved, returned to his seat. He regarded Nathan and Lanie once again.

"Okay, you two. I'm glad to see that you've fitted into the team so well, Miss Rizzo. And, Mr. Long, I think the team loyalty to your colleague is admirable. On the other hand, I don't think it would be very wise for you to try and hide anything from us again. In this instance, we're willing to overlook it, since the

119

end result has worked out well. In the future, we're not likely to be quite so understanding. Do I make myself clear?"

"Yes, sir," Nathan nodded.

"Good. Oh, one final thing . . . Despite what I may have told Miss Long, it really would be very inconvenient if we were forced to expel her. We'd greatly appreciate it if the truth about Miss Rizzo's past didn't become known. I noticed that you've been avoiding getting on film. I'd suggest that you continue that policy."

Lanie nodded, happily. "You got it."

"Thank you." Smiling abruptly, Dr. Thompson added: "I think you've made a wise decision, Nathan, in insisting that Lanie stay part of your team. I suspect she'll be of great help to you all in the future. She's a survivor, and on Mars that will be a very important quality."

Chapter Sixteen

Training was almost over, and they were marking off time to lift off in days instead of weeks. The teams were transferred from Johnson Center in Houston over to the Kennedy Space Center at Cape Canaveral in Florida, and they were all given their first look of the launch site. From here in January, they would ride a torch into space . . .

Kennedy Space Center housed not merely the launch sites and systems, but also the final training headquarters. After the last batch of simulations and emergency tests, there would be one more field exercise, and then it would be their time to leave Earth.

Dr. Thompson led them on their tour of the facilities, from the Vertical Assembly Building, where the shuttles were put together with the boosters, to the pads that they would blast into space from. Incredibly, the site seemed very open and peaceful. Dr. Thompson had grinned when Alice had mentioned this.

"There's even a bird sanctuary out there," he told them, gesturing into the outlands. "They don't seem to mind our occasional launches too much."

"Awesome," Gen muttered. "One of the oldest ways to fly right next to the most up to date."

They were plunged into a madcap round of tests, both physical and mental, and then into the final phases of the program. There was a huge mock-up of the shuttle itself that they were allowed into to familiarize themselves with its workings. The nose housed the crew quarters and living areas. The back, with two huge doors that could open up, was the storage bay for cargo. Inside was a long arm that could be used either to fetch and carry or to take cargo out of the bay and transfer it out into space. The shuttle that they would ride into orbit didn't have a cargo bay. It was a special craft, adapted instead as a large cabin. It was designed specifically to carry a crew into space. Originally it had been used to take up crew to the *Icarus* platform and to bring back astronauts for rests on the Earth. Now, with the To Mars Together project getting into full pace, it was being used to ferry the four hundred plus members of the expedition up to the platform.

One day the team was taken into the shuttle that would carry them, as it stood ready on the launch pad. Dr. Thompson urged them to touch nothing.

"We're getting ready for launch," he explained. "But that's not why you're here. We have to run you through the emergency procedures. God forbid that anything should go wrong, but we have to be ready for all contingencies. Thankfully we have lost very few lives over the years in accidents, but it *has* happened. I'm sure you all know about the tragic *Challenger* disaster. I don't want to get you unduly worried, but we have to consider the possibilities of further problems, and you have to know how to cope with them."

The way into the shuttle was from the launch gantry. The shuttle had been strapped to the giant booster that it would ride most of the way into orbit. Attached on either side of this were small rockets that would drop off a few minutes into the flight. The whole assembly stood clamped in place on Pad 39A, which had been the shuttle launch spot for a number of years now.

The gantry stood to one side like a huge crane. One arm connected to the top of the booster. Lower down, a smaller arm touched the nose of the shuttle, which was pointed up at the stars. Thompson took them up in the elevator to this arm and then led them toward the waiting spacecraft.

"Okay," he said, "here we are on the pad. It's a long way down. You're strapped into the shuttle, and something goes wrong. Say a fire in the cargo bay. What do you do? Run back down the arm toward the elevator? No. Takes too long, and is much too risky." He pointed below the arm. "Plenty of umbilicals connected to the fuel tanks. If one of them catches fire, this whole framework would be a blaze in seconds."

"Thanks," Gen muttered. "Just what I needed to hear."

"They're not pumping fuel now," Karl reassured him. "They wait as late as possible for that."

Dr. Thompson grinned at their unease. "What we need is a fast way down—and we've got one." He led them to what looked like a cable running down at a steep incline to the ground. Clipped to the top end was something that looked like an enclosed child's swing. "It's a variation on the bosun's chair used to get people off sinking ships. Down at the bottom there is a net. You just jump in this and fly. Who's first?"

Alice looked uneasily over the side. It was a long drop, once past the safety barriers. You needed a good head for heights on this trip!

"Me," Lanie grinned, stepping forward. "Better than Disney World." With a wink at the others, she followed Dr. Thompson's instructions and strapped herself into the chair. Then, yelling "Geronimo!" she kicked off.

The gantry disappeared behind her in a second. Apart from the wire overhead that snaked at a slant down to the ground, there was nothing at all but her and the sky — and the fast approaching ground. She felt a moment of panic, and the wind whipping at her hair and clothes. The trees rushed madly up at her, and she spun slightly. Then, abruptly, there was a sudden glimpse of a net, and she hit.

The netting gave just enough to slow her without breaking any bones. Then helping hands reached her, unstrapping her from the seat. She stepped away from it, swaying somewhat from the effects of the ride. Then Sergei cannoned into the net.

One by one, they all ran through the test. Then they rejoined Dr. Thompson on the arm. With a smile, he told them, "We like to show you that first. It gets the blood flowing and warms you up for the rest of it. Now let's go through the rest of the procedures."

The week wore away quickly. Each of the teams got to practice the escape drills. They were shown into the control center and watched as preparations were made to launch the shuttle. They were introduced to Ann Robertson, who they all knew from the news. She'd been one of the first women to work on construction projects in space. A thin black woman, she held herself with easy grace. Streaks of gray now colored her dark hair.

"I'm taking it easy on this mission," she explained. "I'm Cap Com—the person here who'll talk the shuttle crew through the launch." She gestured at the rows of consoles standing in front of the wall-sized monitor screens and maps. "There'll be about fifty people in here, all at these stations, when that baby lifts off. Everyone has something to do." She led them to her own panel. "I get summaries of all the information here," she explained. "And I relay it to the pilots. Basically, I'm a middle man between the control staff and the crew. It gets to be a real madhouse in here during the hours around launchtime."

The shuttle would launch on a routine mission in a few days, and everyone would be allowed to watch it. Dr. Thompson felt it would be good for them to witness the event and settle any doubts they had about the safety measures.

In their spare time, the team explored as much as they could. They took in Disney World, Sea World, and the other sights. They even managed a short trip into the Everglades. Finally, the lift-off time came, and they were all driven out to the observation area. Jessamine and Al were along, as always, filming. They were not alone now, though. They would all watch the launch from special seats constructed at a safe distance. Camera crews from several of the TV and cable channels were covering the launch. There were visiting dignitaries, and plain and simple tourists, all carrying various photographic gear. Some of these even snapped off shots of Nathan and his crew, realizing who they were.

The seven of them had good seats and saw that most

of the other trainee groups were here to observe the launch as well. A loudspeaker intoned the countdown in the background. As it approached the final few minutes, everyone calmed down and settled in to watch. Cameras were trained on the distant site. Then came a short announcement:

"T minus thirty and holding." A short pause, and: "We have a slight problem with a fuel valve." They all knew that such a hold could last a long time — or even cause the delay of the mission for days if it had to be replaced. To pass the time, Sergei extracted another of his long letters from Ludmilla and picked up reading it where he had left off. He was getting a little worried about meeting up with her again. She'd been his girlfriend back in Russia — well, one of them, anyhow. Only she still thought that she was the only one. Sergei wasn't certain if he could break the news to her gently or not. With a little luck, he wouldn't need to. She was on the training program, too, but in Star City, back in Soviet territory. Maybe she'd meet some nice cosmonaut and save Sergei any explaining.

The problem with the shuttle was resolved quickly, and the countdown continued. Shortly before it reached zero, the main booster fired. They could see the wall of flames under the craft, and then, seconds later, heard the sound. At "zero," the gantry swung away, and the shuttle stood free and clear.

Slowly, it began to lift from the pad. Dancing below it, the tremendous power of the rockets heaved it upward. In a blaze of glory, it rose straight into the clear blue sky. Then it began to turn, and to incline, still rising. Clouds of steam trailed behind it, marking its path. Blindingly brilliant, the flames traced their way upward. People in the stands were cheering as the two booster rockets split away from the main tank and fell back toward the ocean. There they would be picked up by waiting boats and brought back to land to be reused.

Finally, the shuttle was gone. The loudspeaker still transmitted information, but no one was really listening now. The excitement of another successful launch was beginning to die down.

Dr. Thompson joined the seven youngsters. "Okay," he told them. "Take the rest of the afternoon off. Meet me at seven tonight at the pad."

"What are we going to do?" Gen joked. "Clean up?"

"No," the astronaut replied. "Another safety test, now that the pad is clear. We're going to drop a mock-up of the shuttle cabin into the bay there. It's a practice session—pretending the shuttle had to ditch into the sea. You just abandon ship. Piece of cake."

Looking unexpectedly worried, Lanie held up her hand hesitantly. "Uh, is this compulsory?" she asked.

Surprised, he nodded. "Of course. You have to be ready for any emergencies. So I'll see you all here tonight. Till then, have fun."

Nathan looked at Lanie with a frown. She seemed very withdrawn and was obviously bothered about something. What could it be? He knew it couldn't be the swim that worried her. She did fine in the pool back in Houston, and had done all of the underwater work with the rest of them. So why did she look so scared?

Chapter Seventeen

That night, a small motor launch took them from the shore out to where the mock-up of the shuttle floated in the bay. It wasn't the full shuttle, simply a nose section containing the crew quarters. There were two helicopters overhead, with large lights turned on, bathing the mock-up in harsh light. Another launch was already there, containing several of the technicians and an emergency diver—just in case. Also in the boat were Jessamine and Al.

Nathan was getting very disturbed. All afternoon, Lanie had been uncharacteristically silent. Now she sat huddled in her jacket, hands jammed tightly in her pockets. She had actually tried to beg off the trip, claiming she wasn't feeling well. She had only come along when Dr. Thompson threatened to take her for medical tests.

The launch docked with the shuttle nose. A technician aboard it reached down to help Dr. Thompson aboard. Then it was the team's turn to clamber in. They had to poke Lanie twice to get her to climb up. Once inside, she moved back into a corner of the cabin, as if trying to hide.

"Okay," Dr. Thompson explained. "The idea here is that the flight's been aborted part way into orbit. You've had to splash down at sea. There's a flooding problem, and you have to evacuate. You all know the routine, so each of you take your seats and get ready. Bill, you and the others wait in the boats. I'll take the inside watch." The technician nodded and disappeared out of the hatch. Dr. Thompson pulled it closed, and then dogged it safely shut. The bright glare of the lights and the noise of the helicopter was now somewhat muted.

Karl and Sergei took the pilots chairs, and strapped in. The rest of them moved to the stations in the crew quarters below the flight deck and took their seats. When they were all ready, Dr. Thompson nodded. "Okay. The shuttle's down in the bay. Water's coming in. Start your evacuation—now!" He snapped on his stop watch, and waited.

Each of them slapped the fast-releases on their safety straps and slid quickly from their seats. Sergei and Karl jumped down from the pilot section, joining the others at the escape hatch. Alice triggered the bolts that ejected the entire door outward, and the glare of the light poured in. Life jackets were stored by the door, and Nathan hastily handed them out.

They strapped into the jackets and hit the small cylinders of air that inflated them. With a slight hissing noise, the Day-Glo orange collars blossomed out.

"Go," Nathan ordered, slapping Karl and Gen. Both leaped out into the air. They had barely hit the water before Noemi and Sergei followed. Then Nathan tapped Alice and Lanie. "Now."

Alice hit the water and sank for a second into the darkness. Her head broke water after a few seconds, buoyed up by the life jacket. Hands reached for her from the launch and she was dragged into the boat, dripping.

She realized suddenly that she was alone. Lanie hadn't jumped.

Nathan glanced uncertainly at Lanie, who had gone completely pale. Shaking her head in terror, she backed away from the door. Nathan looked over to Dr. Thompson for advice, but the astronaut shook his head. "Your decision," he said softly. "You're the leader."

"Come on, Lanie," Nathan called. Again, she shook her head, shrinking back from the door. Her eyes were filled with panic, and she was breathing fast and hard. "It's okay," he said quietly. "There's nothing to worry about." He reached out for her arm, but she slapped him back.

"Get away from me!" she hissed.

"Lanie," he said, trying to be reasonable, "you're going to make us fail the test."

"I don't care," she whispered. "I'm not going out there. I *can't*."

He reached for her again, but she broke completely. Terrified, she punched out, hard. Pain lanced through his stomach as she hit him. He windmilled backward, and suddenly there was no deck under his feet anymore. He hit the water badly, knocking all of the breath out of him.

Then he felt strong arms grabbing him, pulling him out of the water. As soon as he got his breath back, he glanced up at the shuttle hatchway. Lanie was cowering away from the opening, and Dr. Thompson looked far from happy. "Great," Nathan muttered.

Alice tapped his arm. "That's not the worst thing," she told him, pointing. He followed her arm. In the next boat over, Jessamine and Al were getting the whole thing on film.

"If Lanie's stupid behavior doesn't cost us the program," Karl muttered, "then that film is going to. We're sunk whichever way things go."

Don't blame Lanie," Alice snapped back. "The poor thing was petrified with fear.

Karl threw up his arms. "Don't turn into a bunch of bleeding hearts on me! Where was your poor

Chapter Eighteen

Dr. Thompson finally had no choice but to give Lanie a sedative. She refused to move from her safe corner in the shuttle, but didn't struggle as he injected her. After a moment, her eyes slid shut and she pitched forward, fast asleep. He picked her up carefully, amazed at how light she was. Even out cold, she looked badly scared. What on earth was wrong with her?

As he handed her down to the waiting launch, he saw Jessamine talking into the mike. She was getting plenty of great film here—one of the trainees too terrified to jump out of a mock-up . . .

He saw the miserable faces of the others on the team, and knew what they had to be thinking. He'd talk to them tomorrow—they had had enough problems for one night.

Back in the dorms, they split up to go to their rooms. Lanie was being kept in the infirmary overnight till the sedative wore off. The way the rest of them felt, they envied her.

"We're so close," Karl finally exploded. "And that girl is going to wreck it for us!"

132

"Don't blame Lanie," Alice snapped back. "The poor thing was petrified with fear."

"Of getting wet?" sneered Karl. "Give me a break. She's done enough swimming before. What's her problem? Has she got cold feet about going into space, after all?"

"I think we should just wait until tomorrow," Nathan suggested. "Let's give Lanie a chance to tell us what's wrong before we try and judge her. It might just be something really simple."

They all passed a very uneasy night and then reported in for their first session the next day. Lanie entered the room, looking very haggard and sheepish, and she didn't raise her face to even look at the others. Instead, she sat down as far away as she could get.

"Well?" Karl eventually asked, very coldly. "Don't you have something to say?"

"Karl!" Noemi exclaimed angrily. "Give her a chance."

Lanie finally looked up. Her eyes were red with crying, and she looked utterly exhausted. "I'm sorry, guys," she finally managed. "I really am. I screwed up."

Moving over to her side, Alice patted her shoulder. "It's okay," she said sympathetically. "You want to talk about it?"

Lanie stared down at her hands, which were shaking. "I couldn't help it. I just couldn't." Her normal manner of self-assurance was gone completely now. "I never expected we'd have to do that. Never."

"So what's the problem?" Gen asked.

She told them.

* * *

The Chicago skies were dark, and rain hung heavy over the waters of Lake Michigan. Lanie pulled her new leather jacket about her for extra warmth. The wind still crept inside, chilling her bones. The holes in the knees of her jeans didn't help much. She felt like an icicle.

"So what do you say?" Ed Lantry's voice jerked her out of her thoughts. Ed was not exactly her boyfriend — she was only ten, after all, and far too young to be interested in boys. He was fourteen, and handsome in a dangerous way.

"I don't know, Ed," she said slowly. It was one thing to lift a few bags of chips and a six-pack of beer from the deli, but a car was serious stealing.

Ed pointed at the car, idling outside the 7-Eleven. "Come on — here's our chance. Let's cruise the night, kid."

She was still unsure.

The kids in the school all hated her anyway. Because she had no money and tatty clothes. Only Ed didn't treat her like she was a nothing. And if he wanted her help, well . . . he was the only one who ever did.

"Okay," she agreed.

"Right. I knew you were cool." He flashed her a quick grin, and they were off. He slid into the driver's seat, and she went for the passenger side.

At that moment, the owner came out and stopped dead, staring right at them. The sandwiches and doughnuts he'd just bought crashed to the ground, and scattered. "Hey!" he yelled, and ran toward them.

Without thinking, Lanie kicked over the trash can into his legs. Howling, he fell across it. Then she was in the car, and Ed slammed it into reverse. Then they

134

were off, flying through the night.

"Good work," he laughed as he turned on the radio and began to hunt for a rock channel. "Let's party!"

Lanie felt scared. She'd done it. She'd really done it this time. Stealing a car . . . And that guy had looked right at her. Would he remember what she looked like? She had an uneasy vision of the police coming to drag her out of class and throw her into jail.

Right on cue with this thought, the howl of a police siren filled the air.

Panic started to build up in her. Her throat went dry, and she twisted around to paw at Ed's arm. "The cops," she whispered.

"Hey, I got ears," he snapped. Gunning the gas, he sent the car hurtling off down a side road.

The whine of the siren followed them, and she could hear another one ahead of them. Spinning around, she could make out flashing red lights behind them.

"They're gonna get us," she said, her voice catching in fear.

"No they ain't." Ed spun the wheel again, and took the intersection almost on two tires. There were other car headlights and the blare of horns. He switched to the right side of the road and turned into another side street.

Neither of them saw the dead-end sign.

Across the end of the road was a chain-link fence. Unable to stop in time, the car crashed through it, metal screeching. Lanie was flung into the dashboard, and she felt a sharp pain across her chest as she hit. Then she fell backward. She glanced at Ed, who was slumped over the steering wheel, his face bloody.

The car had slowed and was skidding sideways. As

Lanie struggled with the wheel, she realized that they were on wood, not a road.

A dock! They'd broken through onto a dock by the lake.

The car hit the wooden safety fence, still skidding. The wood splintered, raining about them. Teetering, the car then tipped and fell, straight toward the waiting waters of the lake.

Lanie screamed as the car slammed into the water. The shock rocked her, and the car began to sink. The dark waters closed over the windows, and the blackness settled about her. As she scrambled for the door handle, there was a soft thump.

The car was on the bottom of the lake.

Struggling with the door, Lanie realized that she was still screaming. She almost bit through her tongue as she clamped her mouth shut, fighting back the nauseating waves of panic that descended upon her. Try as she might, the door wouldn't open. She was trapped here, in the mud on the bottom of the lake.

How long would it be before she suffocated to death? Fighting back the terror, she tried to think. It was no use. She just wanted to scream, to flail about in panic. She could see nothing at all in the blackness. The only sound was the ragged noise of Ed's breathing.

The interior light! She fumbled about, scratching at the roof of the car, breaking her nails. Then she found the switch and clicked it on. The ghostly light flooded the cramped interior but didn't do anything to relieve her fears. The car was embedded in the mud. She could see a few inches out the windows, but that was all. The gloom absorbed all light beyond that. Inside the car, all she could see was Ed's limp body, blood still trickling down his scalp.

She tried the door again, with no more luck. Vaguely, she knew that the water pressure outside was greater than the air pressure inside the car, and that as a result she couldn't open the door. There had to be an answer, but she didn't know what it was.

Her breathing was getting louder. Suddenly aware of this, she wondered if they could have used up all of the air already. She began to choke, trying to get a lungful of fresh air. It seemed to be missing completely. Spots swam across her eyes, and she felt very faint. She felt very giddy too, and in a blinding rush of panic, she passed out.

Later she awoke. Her head swam, and she felt really sick. In a sudden wave of terror, she remembered about the car and shot upright. Looking around quickly, she saw she was in a hospital.

Leaning to the left, she saw a cop, watching her with a certain amount of pity. Then her strength left her, and she collapsed back into the pillow.

She was in real trouble this time. The police had managed to locate her mother. Mrs. Johnson arrived drunk, insisting that her child was a good kid and would never steal a car. Lanie cringed. Her mother always managed to embarrass her.

Slowly, Lanie pieced together what had happened. The cop who watched over her was a nice guy, with kids of his own. He told her that the squad car had chased her to the lake and immediately called for help. Divers had gone down to the sunken car and fished both Ed and Lanie out. Both of them had suffered from minor oxygen starvation, but little else.

After a few days Lanie had recovered. Then had come the ordeal of the court. The judge at her hearing had believed she'd been led astray by Ed, and that what she needed most was good supervision. He gave Lanie probation and let her out.

That night, Lanie had jerked awake from a nightmare. She sat there on the mattress that served as her bed, shivering in the darkness. She had dreamed of falling into the river again, and of the blackness closing in about her. It was over an hour before she got back to sleep.

Lanie grew up, but that nightmare never left her. At least once a week, she would awaken in absolute terror, gasping for breath. Then she would lie awake in the darkness, too terrified of dying to go back to sleep.

"It's no good," she told the others. "I can't do it. I never thought it'd be a problem—I mean, there's not even a puddle on the surface of Mars! It's just . . . when I looked out of that hatchway at the dark and the water, I just couldn't do it. I'm sorry I let you down, but I can't . . ." She broke off, burying her face in her hands.

Alice and Noemi both held her. They could feel the wracking sobs that shook Lanie's thin body. It was quite obvious that their friend was in trouble.

And so was the team.

Chapter Nineteen

Dr. Thompson had been polite but firm about the whole matter. Lanie would have a second chance at the evacuation test after the Iceland trip. If she refused again to go through with it, he would have no option but to recommend her dismissal from the team.

This cast a huge shadow over what would otherwise have been an exciting time. Whenever they talked about the final field test in Iceland, they were thrilled with an impending sense of adventure. Then one look at Lanie's haunted face and their own joy evaporated. After all, how could they really prepare themselves into this trip knowing that when they came back, Lanie would most likely be cut?

"Iceland's the logical choice to test the ground systems," Karl told the others. "It's a volcanic country, with very little vegetation. In many ways, it's similar to Mars."

"In the late eighties," added Sergei, "a group of Soviet and American space artists went to Iceland to paint the landscape, for inspiration on what Mars might look like." He shrugged. "I guess the habit caught on."

Noemi shuddered. "I don't know why you're so happy about going. Tramping about in the ice and snow doesn't sound so great to me."

139

"Hey, it's not that bad," Karl told her. "Actually, at this time of the year, it's colder in Chicago than Iceland."

"So why is it called Iceland, then?"

"Advertising?" laughed Sergei. "No, it's true: Iceland was discovered after Greenland, and settled by the Vikings. Because it's so volcanic, Iceland is much better land than Greenland. So the colonists mislabeled both places, hoping that future settlers would head for Greenland and not steal the best spots!"

"Smart," Gen muttered.

"If you think that's weird," Sergei told him, "wait till you see this place. I've seen prints of the artwork the Soviet artists painted."

The island lived up to Sergei's boasting. The team was part of a contingency of seventy people flown in for the simulations that would be run. NASA had rented out an entire hotel in the capital city of Reykjavik, and the seven of them were surprised at how comfortable it was. The weather was cool, but hardly as cold as they had been expecting. The town was small—but the only one of any size at all on the entire island—and all the buildings were brick or stone.

"Not much wood grows here," Sergei pointed out. "But there's lots of stone!"

The natives were mostly a cheerful bunch, and most of them could speak fluent English—with a Scandinavian accent. The only drawback that any of them could find to the entire place was that the prices in the shops were so high. Even Noemi had second thoughts about buying souvenirs.

"Don't forget," Sergei lectured, "it's almost all got to be imported. That's why everything's so expensive."

But they had very little time for sight-seeing. They were only scheduled for a week's stay, and then the next teams would be brought in. Once the technicians had everything prepared, the youngsters were loaded into a bus and driven out to the chosen sites. As usual, Jessamine and Al were close behind, though even the thought of more filming couldn't dampen their spirits.

The scenery was beautiful. Huge mountains, capped with snow; roadside lakes and pools; brilliantly green grass, but virtually no plants or trees. And, every now and then, spumes of geysers.

"Iceland is totally volcanic," Sergei explained. As the geologist member of the team, he'd really done his homework. "As you know, the surface of the Earth is like a series of plates that move. In California, for example, the slow collision of two of these plates forms your San Andreas Fault. But here in Iceland, the opposite is happening. Two plates are pulling apart. At Thingvellir, there's a huge chasm caused by this, and so are all the volcanoes. Iceland has over two hundred. But don't worry — only thirty of those are still active."

"Great," muttered Gen. "Let's hope we don't get too close to any active ones."

"It might be good practice," Nathan offered with a straight face. "After all, Mount Olympus on Mars is a huge volcano. Maybe we should start small, here in Iceland."

Gen sighed. "I wonder if it's too late to switch to a Venus mission?"

The bus drew to a halt, and their Icelandic guide stood up. He was tall, with long raven-black hair down to his shoulders, and an infectious grin. "Here we are at Sprengisandur," he told them. "My name is Ragnar

Hilmarsson, and I'll be happy to answer any questions you may have."

"Why's this place called—what was it, Spingy . . . ?" one of the other youngsters called out.

"Sprengisandur," Ragnar answered. "It means *exploding sands.*"

"Uh . . ." the kid said, looking out of the window. "What does it do? Blow up when you step on it?"

"Nothing so dramatic, I'm afraid. When the original colonists rode across this area on horseback, the hoof-beats sounded like small explosions. You're not likely to have that trouble."

"It's the volcanic sands," Sergei explained, glad to be able to make use of his geological studies. "The grains are bigger than normal sand, and when you walk on them, they rub together, producing strange sounds. In Hawaii, they call it *barking sands* and in the Gobi Desert it's the *singing sands.*"

Gen grinned. "Cool. But since the sands make so much noise, how about making a little less yourself?" He ducked the mock-punch Sergei threw at him. Still clowning around, they disembarked and paused to look around. It was wild and desolate, with rocks and sand stretching into the jagged cliffs and mountains.

"It *does* look like the pictures of the surface of Mars," Alice commented. "All it needs is a red tint."

"Hence the reason we chose it for practice," Dr. Thompson told them. He grinned. "Okay, Mr. Muller—here's your chance for some fun. You get to play with the Mars Rover—but carefully, please."

A rare smile creased the German youth's face. If there was one passion in Karl's life, it was driving. The Rovers were weird-looking vehicles by any normal standards, but they were not designed as sports cars. Bulky and round-bodied, with projecting computer-controlled cargo arms and huge wheels, they would be the only vehicles on Mars to start with, and Karl was eager to gain his qualifications to drive them.

Each was fitted with a small CB radio, vitally important for work on Mars. It would be their lifeline to the colony in case anything went wrong. Gen could field strip and repair them in fifteen minutes.

Al started filming as Gen and Karl checked out the Rover. Since there were no garages or repair shops on the road either here or on Mars, before any Rover was taken out, it was thoroughly checked. Then, with a whoop, the two boys roared off, scattering sand and dust behind them, at an impressive twenty miles per hour.

Dr. Thompson laughed. "I like to see people who enjoy their work."

Meanwhile, the rest of them had been given their assignments. Noemi and Alice were to test one of the sample kits they'd be using on Mars. It was vitally important to find good growing soil for the crops, and volcanic soil was the best possible, filled with the minerals plants need to grow well. Nathan and Sergei were to practice with the filtration systems that would be used on Mars. Dust storms occasionally raced across the surface of the planet, and it would be vital to prevent any dust getting into the domes of the colony. Hence the need for a reliable filter system in all airlocks. With the sand here, they could test out the efficiency of the units for Mars.

Which left Lanie. Dr. Thompson had taken into account that all of the tests here would be filmed by Jessamine Jarvis. Lanie had been assigned to space-suit testing. The Martian atmosphere was extremely thin, and to move around on the surface, the colonists would need reliable, workable pressure suits. Since they had to perform over a long period of time and under a variety of conditions, the suits were being tested thoroughly.

Lanie grumbled a little — it was like living in a can — but she knew the main reason she'd been given this assignment. When she had the helmet on, its reflective faceplate would prevent her face from showing. Jessamine could film all she wanted, but no one would recognize Lanie within the suit.

She had to get back on the bus to be suited up. Thankfully, this wasn't going to be filmed, because she had to strip down for the suiting. First on was a thermal one-piece undergarment to keep her warm. It fastened up the front with Velcro strips and was thoughtfully provided with a little plastic bag. There were no rest rooms on Mars — and it would take too long to get out of the suit even if there were. Once you were locked in, it would be for several hours at a time. This was just a test suit — the real Mars suits would have a more complex waste recycling system built into them. But NASA had no intention of risking a very expensive Mars suit for the practice runs, and Lanie would have to put up with the discomfort.

Alice and Noemi helped her with the next part of the suiting up. Wrinkling her nose at the design, Noemi muttered, "Mars fashions! Ugh."

It wouldn't win any awards for beauty — but it would keep them alive. Lanie slipped into the bottom section, which looked like very baggy trousers, with a huge waist. Then came the boots. Alice checked the seals, to ensure that there were no possible leaks. When she was certain that was fine, Lanie moved to the board that held the upper section of the suit. She had to bend to get up inside it, and then Alice checked the seals between that and the bottom half.

Noemi helped Lanie don the gloves, then checked their seals. One leak anywhere in the suit could be lethal on Mars. Next, over the body of the suit came the oxygen backpack. This was connected up with thin but strong corrugated piping to the suit intakes, and tested to make certain the air flow was unblocked and the tanks filled. Then came the skullcap that held the radio mouthpiece and earphones, Lanie's only link with the outside once she was fully suited. It was connected to the electrical systems inside the suit, and the frequency changes could be made only by Lanie using her chin to tap the controls in the neckband of the suit. Once again, they checked that the radio was working. Then, with the oxygen switched on, Alice helped Lanie into the helmet. With this sealed, Lanie was living totally within the suit.

"How's it feel?" asked Noemi into the hand-held radio.

"Like I'm a sardine," Lanie's voice crackled over the speaker. "It's cramped in here. But all systems go."

While Alice and Noemi watched, Lanie climbed out of the van with care. Then she gave a little jump in the air, to test the systems out. When she hit the ground with her feet, the others hear little popping noises. For a second they were worried that something had gone wrong, but then they realized it was simply the "exploding sands."

145

Dr. Thompson left the team. The bus would be taking the next group on to Tungnafellsjokull, an area that was very like the polar cap on Mars. On its way back, it would collect Alpha team and check their results. For now, there were just the seven of them at work, and Jessamine and Al filming whatever went on.

Lanie found that it wasn't too bad inside the suit after all. The temperature was kept constant, and she couldn't feel the strong wind outside. She was expected to help with the experiments of the other four, to see how practical the suit would be to use on Mars. Despite its apparent bulkiness, it didn't weigh a whole lot, and the gloves proved to be no problem when picking things up and handing them to the others.

Jessamine was conscientiously getting as much as possible onto film. In fact, the tests were proceeding very well. Al was taping the experiments that Sergei and Nathan were conducting and seemed to be enjoying things. Feeling slightly bored, Jessamine walked off to do a little sight-seeing.

Al had proven to be quite a nice guy, unlike his boss. His easygoing grin was genuine, and he took everything as a matter of course. Jessamine yelled at him as often as she did at other people, but he had never said a word back to her. When he was certain that the camera was off, Nathan had asked Al once 'How he could stand her.'

"Lot's of practice," Al joked. "She's not so bad, really. I could tell you some stories — but I wouldn't want them to get around the grapevine even on Mars!"

He didn't hold Jessamine's views about the Mars project being a waste of money and time, but she was the boss, and it was her story that he was filming. In fact, he admitted a certain sympathy for the kids. He had three of his own and showed their pictures every chance he could get. They were seven, five, and two, and he was immensely proud of them. "Who knows," he joked to Alice, as she took another batch of soil samples. "They may wind up being the first colonists on Venus!"

"Well," she answered, "they'd get to practice somewhere a bit warmer than this — the temperature on the surface there is over four hundred degrees."

"Good for a tan," Noemi cracked.

Inside the suit, Lanie was cut off from all of the banter. All she could see was that the others seemed to be having fun. All she could hear was her own breathing, unless the radio was being used. Under different circumstances, that wouldn't have bothered her — she was used to being alone, after all. But with her being thrown off the project when she returned . . . She felt sick at heart. Testing out the suit might have been fun, otherwise. As it was, she simply couldn't get into it. And the more the others looked like they were enjoying themselves, the more she was reminded that they would be going to Mars, and not her.

All because she was afraid of the open water.

Annoyed at herself, she wandered off farther than she had expected. She had a vague idea of testing the suit out among the rocks when she stumbled across the unexpected once again. Iceland was full of surprises, and here was one of them — a jet-black lake hidden amidst the boulders in the foothills. In the shadows of the large rocks, barely any light reached the surface of the waters, let alone penetrated below.

It brought to mind the terrifying darkness of Lake

Michigan, and Lanie started to shudder as the memories flooded back again.

"Hey, Lanie" came Nathan's voice over the radio. "Head up! Al's coming over to get some footage of you. Look pretty for the camera, okay?"

Snapped out of her morbid introspection, Lanie looked around. Steadying his camera on his shoulder, Al was perching atop one of the rocks by the small lake and filming in her direction. She waved, and started to walk toward him.

He shifted his footing, trying to get a slightly different angle. As Lanie watched, she saw that a piece of the stone ledge shattered and skidded out from under him. Al's arms windmilled as he tried to keep his balance, but without luck. His mouth opened and he fell backward, into the blackness of the lake.

Lanie rushed toward the spot, expecting to see him come stumbling out, dripping and furious. Instead, the ripples of his fall slowly began to dissipate, and there was no sign of movement.

The camera equipment! Lanie suddenly realized that the weight of it must be pinning him down. And if he'd hit his head, he could be drowning right now!

Staring in horror at the black waters, Lanie knew that she was his only hope. The others wouldn't be able to get there in time to save him—even if they could go under and find him in the gloom.

But she couldn't go into the darkness . . . she just couldn't!

Chapter Twenty

She was frozen to the spot for a few seconds, aware that Al was probably dying slowly under the water. She wanted to go in and help him, but she was paralyzed in fear, impossible for her to move.

Nathan's voice snapped her out of it. "How's the filming going?"

Fighting back the nausea of her fear, Lanie triggered the radio link. "Emergency!" she snapped. "Al's fallen in a small lake, and he hasn't come up. Get help, fast. I'm going after him."

She switched on the light built into her suit helmet, closed her eyes for a second, and then, before she could think twice about it, she plunged forward, into the lake.

Her entire body was shaking in terror, but she refused to give in. It was a good job that these suits had plumbing in them, though. The black waters closed over her head, and the only thing she could see was a small patch of light in front of her feet where her light shone. It starkly illuminated small boulders and tiny tendrils of plants.

She felt physically sick with the fear. Pictures and memories of being trapped in the car kept flashing into her mind. She wanted to scream, to throw up, to just curl into a ball and die. But if she did, then Al would die — and it would be her fault.

"We're on our way," she heard Nathan say, and she sighed in relief. Fixing on the reality of the others helped to push back the horror of what she was doing.

"I can't see him yet," she reported, her voice shaking. "But I must be getting close."

The small circle of light she cast was weaving about in the lapping waters. Shadows were sharp, and the image really poor. Maybe she'd not even be able to find him and . . .

Then the light flashed over him, and she jerked her head back to center on him. He must have hit his head as he fell, because she could see something dark floating slowly away from the back of his scalp. Trickles of blood.

She struggled against the resistance of the water to reach him. She could tell that he wasn't breathing. As she'd figured, the weight of all his equipment was holding him down.

Finally, she was by his side. "Got him!" she snapped.

"Good," she heard Nathan say. "I'm at the lakeside now, but can't see anything. How is he?"

"He's unconscious." She couldn't feel anything when she reached for his chest, but that could be because her gloves were too thick, not because his heart had stopped.

In the gloom, she couldn't see how to release all of the straps to free him from his gear. And she couldn't move all of his weight. She reached down to the small tool kit stored in the leg of her suit, and pulled out the pincers. Fighting back her fears, she sliced through every strap she could.

Then she grabbed Al and started back for the surface the way she had come.

As she struggled, she discovered that her fears for Al's life were battering down her own terrors. She was going to make it! If only Al was going to make it, too . . .

It seemed like forever that she pushed against the water, forcing her way step by step back up to the shore. Then, finally, her head broke the surface, out into the blinding sun, and she felt other hands grabbing at Al and lifting his heaviness from her arms.

Nathan and Alice dragged Al's limp body from Lanie, and struggled him to the shore. Noemi and Sergei had cleared a patch of sand while Jessamine stood by, eyes wide, wringing her hands together helplessly.

"No heartbeat, no respiration," Nathan said, testing. "He's in bad shape."

"CPR," Noemi replied firmly. Pushing Nathan aside, she bent to begin. Tilting back Al's head, she checked that his tongue was clear of his throat, to prevent choking. Then she took a deep breath, pressing her mouth over his and exhaling. Then again. And again.

"Nothing," Nathan said after a few more attempts. Noemi nodded, and then pressed both palms over Al's heart. Five sharp thrusts, then two more breaths into his mouth. Then five more bangs on his chest, and two more breaths.

With a convulsive jerk, Al spat water out. Choking, he struggled about, and Noemi helped him to vomit out the water he'd swallowed. With a whooping cough, Al started to breathe again.

Alice bent over to look at the bleeding patch on his head. "We'll need a dressing on this," she said. "I'll get the first aid kit."

"And one of the coats," Nathan suggested. "Shock's going to set in otherwise. And that can kill him just as sure as drowning."

Alice nodded and ran back to the equipment dump the bus had left. Jessamine hovered over the others.

"Is he okay?" she asked. Nathan looked up, and for the first time, he saw something other than the lust for a scoop in her eyes.

"So far," he told her. "He's breathing, and his heart is weak, but steady. We have to keep him warm and get him to a hospital, fast."

"But the bus isn't coming back for hours. And it would take too long to call for help."

Lanie had managed to remove her helmet and heard this last comment. "We don't have to wait for help," she said. "It's already on its way."

Puzzled, Jessamine asked, "What are you talking about?"

Lanie pointed. Looking around, Jessamine saw Karl and Gen driving over in the Rover. "Sergei called them back as soon as he knew something was wrong. That Rover's the only thing that can get Al to hospital in time."

They had to carry Al out of the large boulders. Then they loaded him onto the back of the Rover, wrapping him in every coat they could spare. Cannibalizing what they could from the equipment, they strapped him firmly down.

"Go as fast as you can," Nathan told Karl. "But get there in one piece, okay?"

Karl smiled briefly. "Trust me," he promised.

"We do."

Nodding, Karl and Gen gunned the engine, and shot off as fast as the Rover could take them, heading back to Reykjavik.

But would they manage it in time?

Chapter Twenty-one

The moon was full, and the sky cloudless. Above them, the stars burned in all of their glories. In the waters of the bay, the small launch rocked slightly. Lying back with a huge grin on her face, Lanie pushed the wet hair out of her face and howled in happiness.

She'd beaten the fear! After the walk in the lake, jumping into the ocean bay wearing a life jacket had been a snap.

Alice patted her arm, and Noemi gave her a hug. Karl, more reserved as usual, settled for a brief shake of her hand. Gen slapped her a high five.

"All right, Rizzo!" he crowed. "You're one of us!"

"Yeah," she said smugly. "Now you're really stuck with me. I'm going to Mars!"

Sergei gave a mock shudder. "A decision I'm certain we'll live to regret," he announced. But he winked, and punched her gently.

Nathan smiled, too. "Glad to see you're with us. Somehow it wouldn't be the same if we had been forced to leave you behind."

"No," Noemi agreed. "It would have been too quiet."

Al snorted as he turned off his new camera. "Not much chance of that with you kids." He was none the worse for his experience — save for a tender spot that remained on the back of his head. His stay in the hospital had ended just two days ago, and he and Jessamine were back to work on the documentary again.

Al had thanked them all for saving his life, but especially Lanie. He realized what she had gone through. He managed to get her alone, and handed her a small

154

gift-wrapped parcel.

"What did you do this for?" Lanie asked, fighting back her tears. "You're crazy. We all helped out."

"Open it," he suggested. "It's something for the team."

Shrugging, Lanie tore off the wrapping. Inside was a video cassette. Puzzled, she looked up at Al, who grinned.

"It's the master tape of all the foul-ups you guys made. I told Jessamine that it's at the bottom of that lake in Iceland. I sort of figured you and the others might like to have it." He grinned again. "It means we'll have to re-shoot the footage, of course — but it'll give you a chance to get it right. I think that'll happen this time, don't you?"

Clutching the tape tightly, she nodded, and ran to find the others.

That night, they ceremonially erased the tape.

Like Al had said, it would mean further filming — but they were certain that there would be no goof-ups to embarrass NASA this time around. And the first thing they had filmed was Lanie's triumphant escape at night from the shuttle mock-up.

Jessamine, true to form, never mentioned the problem, or the lost tape. Instead, she simply had them run through all their paces again. But, as she was about ready to leave for California and the final edit of the documentary, she stopped by to see them.

"I still think that NASA is crazy to be sending you kids to Mars," she told them flatly. "But . . . well, if they *have* to send children, I can't think of any bunch that's better qualified." Abruptly, she held out her hand. "The best of luck to all of you."

Nathan shook her hand and managed a smile.

155

Her film aired two days before launch. It was called *Stars In Their Eyes, Mars In Their Hearts*. While not exactly unbiased, it was nowhere near as bad as any of them had feared. Lanie had kept out of focus almost all of the time, to their relief. And there wasn't a single instance of any of them making an error. At the end of the documentary, Jessamine appeared on tape, summing up.

"NASA's use of juveniles on their To Mars Together project remains, at least to this reporter, a rather dubious decision. But, having spent time with them all, I have to confess that they do give even me cause for hope. Perhaps with their input, Mars may be able to become a second home for the human race—a community that transcends the barriers of race, creed, and culture. The youngsters who I had dealings with proved to be brave, resourceful and inspiring. I join with the rest of humanity in wishing them a safe voyage and a pleasant haven at their journey's end. May they all find what they are looking for."

Epilogue

It had been a long, hard struggle for them all. They had all been forced to shake off something of their pasts, to adjust to a future that would be vastly different from anything they had ever known. But they could do it. They *would* do it!

Nathan glanced about the shuttle cabin at the members of his team. A great group, he knew. They had come through this far in good shape, but there were still plenty of challenges ahead. The shuttle had left the Earth's atmosphere behind now. It would be heading for the *Icarus* platform.

The usual flurry of activity about the platform would calm down to enable the shuttle to dock. Somewhere, people were getting the transfer tunnel ready so that the seven of them could leave the shuttle and enter the platform in space.

Very shortly, they would hear the ringing sound of the metal connections being made, and they would start on the second phase of their journey to Mars.

Mars! So close at last. Nathan took another look around. Gen, Karl, Sergei, Noemi, Lanie, and Alice . . . His team. They were ready for Mars. They were ready for *anything*. Considering what lay ahead of them still, that was a good thing. . . .

Can Nathan, Karl, Lanie, Noemi, Gen, Alice and Sergei survive the hidden dangers aboard the orbiting space platform Icarus? *Find out in the next action-packed adventure:*
THE YOUNG ASTRONAUTS #3: SPACE BLAZERS

For more information about The Young Astronaut Council, or to start a Young Astronaut Chapter in your school, write to:

THE YOUNG ASTRONAUT COUNCIL
1211 Connecticut Avenue, N.W.
Suite 800
Washington, D.C. 20036

Follow the odyssey . . .

The YOUNG ASTRONAUTS

Blast off with Nathan, Sergei, Lanie, Noemi, Alice, Gen and Karl on their future adventures in outerspace—a new one every other month!

November, 1990:
**THE YOUNG ASTRONAUTS #3:
SPACE BLAZERS**

January, 1991:
**THE YOUNG ASTRONAUTS #4:
DESTINATION: MARS**

March, 1991:
**THE YOUNG ASTRONAUTS #5:
SPACE PIONEERS**

May, 1991:
**THE YOUNG ASTRONAUTS #6:
CITIZENS OF MARS**

Look for them at your local bookstore.
Be sure to collect the whole series including:
**THE YOUNG ASTRONAUTS
THE YOUNG ASTRONAUTS #2:
READY FOR BLAST OFF**